GW00818505

TIME IN THE TIDE

TIME IN THE TIDE

John Hepburn

To Gina,
Don't lose your love of the sea. Happy reading

Book Guild Publishing
Sussex, England

First published in Great Britain in 2005 by
The Book Guild Ltd
25 High Street
Lewes, East Sussex
BN7 2LU

Typesetting in Palatino by
Keyboard Services, Luton, Bedfordshire

Printed in Great Britain by
CPI Bath

A catalogue record for this book is available from
The British Library

ISBN 1 85776 928 7

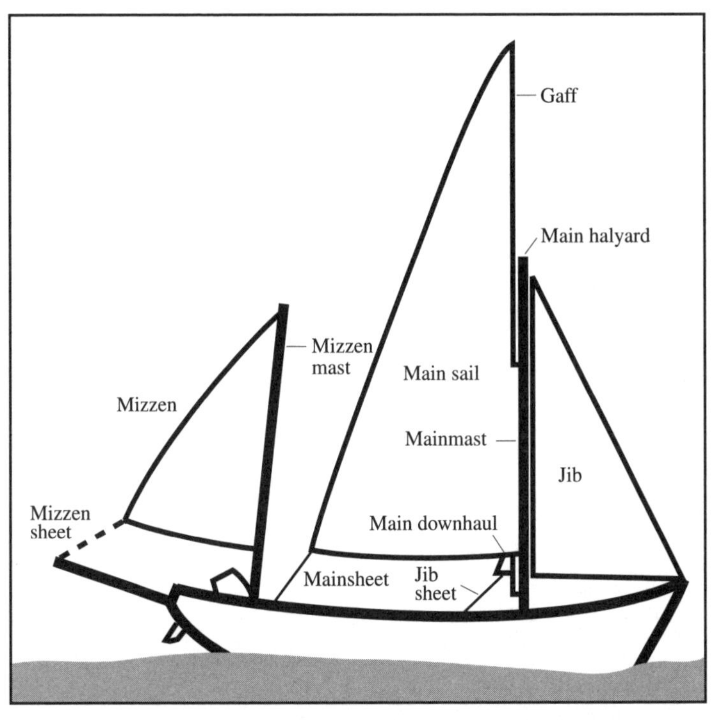

The more important parts of a Drascombe Lugger

Key to map of Plymouth and its estuaries.
Items appear in the order they do in the story.

1 River Tamar
2 Devil's Point
3 Barn Pool
4 Torpoint
5 The Hoe
6 Big wall on top of the hill (Stadden Heights)
7 Drake's Island
8 Breakwater Fort
9 Breakwater
10 Big bridge with funny arches (Brunel's 1869 Albert Bridge)
11 Saltash
12 River Lynher
13 Hamoaze
14 Wearde Quay
15 Uncle Jim's mooring
16 Kingsand
17 The Bridge (a channel, not a bridge)
18 Cawsand Bay
19 Fort Picklecombe
20 The Sound
21 Bovisand
22 The Narrows
23 Jennycliffe Bay
24 Old Royal Western Yacht Club site
25 Pascoe and Brothers' Yard
26 Plymouth
27 The Eddystone (off the map)
28 Library, museum and art gallery
29 Calstock (off the map)
30 Wivelscombe Lake
31 Ince Castle
32 Morwellham (off the map)
33 Millbrook
34 St John's Lake
35 Forder Creek
36 Flooded meadow
37 St Stephen's Church
38 Newton Ferrers (off the map)
39 The Mewstone (off the map)
40 River Yealm (off the map)
41 Henn Point
42 Jupiter Point
43 Beggar's Island
44 River Tavy (off the map)
45 Bere Ferrers (off the map)
46 Marina in Plymouth
47 The Barbican

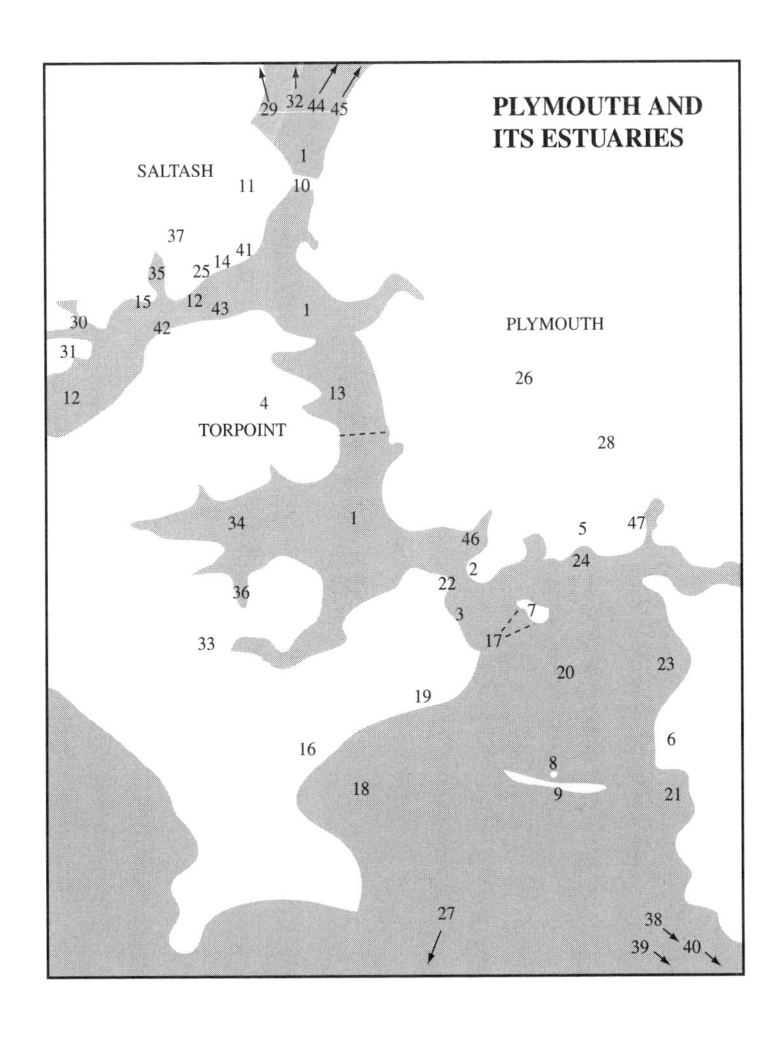
PLYMOUTH AND
ITS ESTUARIES
29
32
44
45
1
SALTASH
11
10
37
41
14
25
35
15
12
43
1
30
42
31
12
PLYMOUTH
26
13
4
TORPOINT
28
34
1
5
47
46
24
2
22
36
7
3
17
33
20
23
19
6
16
8
18
9
21
27
38
39
40

1

What did it matter that we had a boring old project to complete during the holidays? At least we were on holiday, and determined to make it one to remember. Well, we certainly succeeded there, but not quite in the way we would have liked, and there were certainly bits I would rather forget – but I'm getting ahead of myself.

There were four of us spending the summer with my Uncle Jim and Aunt Liz in Saltash, on the Cornwall side of the Tamar. Cousin Carol, our two friends from school, Christine and Judy, and I were all separated from parents overseas, but there was some compensation in being able to stick together. The penalty to pay for that was The Victorian Project.

Everyone was to do one. As we were to be together we had hit on the idea of combining on 'The River Tamar during the Reign of Queen Vic' – with a bit of organisation, we reckoned we could get away with not having to work too hard. Miss Welford, our history teacher, had seen through that, as we found when we arrived in Saltash the previous day. She and Uncle Jim had plotted to ensure that we all had plenty to do. He was un-friend for at least half an hour when we found out. But the silver lining to that particular cloud was that he'd agreed that we should do lots of sailing. In fact we were working while sailing that very afternoon – the first day of holidays. That was the day we met David Williams, who contrary to initial impressions turned out a very good egg, and certainly on the side of the angels.

We'd had a good beat down the Tamar with me in charge of Uncle Jim's Drascombe Lugger *Evenstar*. The ebb was running strongly our way, but we were getting close to Devil's Point (which gave Uncle Jim a chance to remind us we needed to read up about Royal William Yard) and it was time to tack. A small red boat, a sort of dory with a little lid, had been slowly overtaking us for the last few minutes and was now 50 metres on the weather quarter, making me worry that tacking might be dangerous.

Uncle Jim, however, had been keeping a lookout, all appearances to the contrary. 'I should think he'll keep out of your way,' he said. 'He must have seen you, he's been there the last five minutes, and if he has any sense, he'll know you've got to tack now. But just in case, we'll give him a quick blast on the fog horn, and Sally, you stick your arm out, then we'll go.'

'Ready about,' I said. Carol unjammed the port jib sheet and Christine picked up the starboard. Judy gave a hoot on the brass fog horn, I put my arm out and looked at the man in the speedboat who nodded back. It was going to be all right. 'Lee ho!' I sang out and pushed the tiller to port. *Evenstar* swung through the eye of the wind and settled down heading towards Mount Edgecombe, with Devil's Point slipping past the port beam 25 metres away, safely beyond the three or four fishing lines fanning out from it, as Christine sheeted the jib home.

But it was not all right. The little red boat was now coming straight for us; the driver did not seem to have noticed our 100-degree alteration at all. That the situation was pretty hairy was proved by the speed with which Uncle Jim appeared by my side, and the volume of his bellowed 'Ahoy!'

Before he had a chance to take the tiller, though, the red boat's driver, probably alerted by the shout, saw us, swung his wheel to starboard and revved up. The sudden change of course heeled him hard to starboard, and he passed perhaps a bit less than a couple of boats' lengths clear. He was obviously very angry. Even though his words were drowned by the roar of his engine, his shaken fist was good enough evidence of his feelings.

Uncle Jim had already relaxed into his normal unexcited and apparently lethargic manner. 'Well, what's wound him up, I wonder?' he muttered.

I, on the other hand, was really cross. He had certainly seen my signal, and surely his nod had indicated that he understood I was going to tack, and now he had made me look like a dangerous helmsman who tacks into someone's water without looking.

'Hello, he's coming back, and I don't think it's to apologise,' remarked Christine, who had the best view to starboard.

'I think you're right,' said Uncle Jim. 'He can't really mean to ram us, but he's giving a good impression of trying. Helm up! Let the main go, Christine.'

As he said it, he unjammed the mizzen sheet. With main and mizzen free, there was nothing to stop *Evenstar* bearing away, and the heel to windward as the weight came off the sails helped. She swung through 90 degrees in under a boat's length. The other boat had also done a hard turn to starboard, sending a curtain of spray in our direction. Uncle Jim took charge.

'Let's get her sailing again. Here, I'll do the main, you do the mizzen,' he told me.

I luffed back onto course. 'Do you think he's trying to sink us?'

'He's turning again,' said Judy. 'I wish we had a shotgun, I'd blow him out of the water.' As always, Judy's refusal to submit to what she felt was unfair pressure cheered us up.

'No, that was done to frighten us, he altered just before we did,' said Uncle Jim. 'Obviously he feels hard done by, and that we need a lesson, but I think we can teach him one, if, as I guess, his next pass is astern. Christine, dig out the mackerel line and the polythene bag we've got for the fish, please, and then change places with me.'

Working with unusual haste on the lee side, Uncle Jim hooked a corner of the bag on the mackerel spinner, put it over the side and paid it out. The small weight on the line kept it below the water but just visible. He dropped the rowing crutch in its hole, passed the line through it and sat on the centreboard case with a good bight of slack line between his fingers.

As he had predicted, the red boat closed fast and made a last-minute course change to pass close astern, where he went right over the plastic carrier bag that Uncle Jim had veered to the precise distance behind us. The fishing line went taut then slack and the red boat lost way as its outboard went quiet.

'That taught him,' crowed Judy, becoming vigorous in her delight in revenge, but she shut up at a growled 'Quiet, there's more to come,' from Uncle Jim as he recovered the mackerel line, with a small grunt of disappointment that the spinner had gone with the plastic bag.

'OK, Sally, gybe round and we'll go alongside. Carol, fenders please, on the port side. Judy, can you dig out that thickish blue line from the locker you're sitting on, please?'

The red boat was now lying stern to the wind, while the driver was trying ineffectually to restart the engine. So he did not notice *Evenstar* until I put her alongside his port side.

'Very, very neat, Sally,' whispered Uncle Jim, which cheered me up no end, and then more loudly, 'Afternoon, old chap, got a problem? Heard your engine stop. Sounded like you've picked up something in the prop. Filthy river this, all sorts of things floating in it to trap the unwary, bits of rope, plastic bags, you name it.'

I hadn't realised how devious Uncle Jim was, and even then did not fully appreciate just how crafty he could be. He leant over the side, his hands resting on the other's gunwales, keeping the two boats apart.

The man turned, startled, and then aghast. Uncle Jim is a big man and could be expected to be somewhat irate; indeed we were astonished at how friendly he seemed. 'Can't stop here, you know. There's a whole bunch of minesweepers about to come round the corner, and the Queen's Harbour Master will be less than pleased to find you cluttering up the fairway. Best we give you a tow over to Barn Pool, over there,' he indicated over his shoulder, 'and then we can get you sorted out in peace, OK?'

'Er, well, um, I don't know,' the other mumbled, and then looked past his starboard quarter to where the Queen's Harbour Master's launch was indeed leading a small squadron of minesweepers past the Hoe. 'Yes, please.'

'And at no charge,' said Uncle Jim, as he let *Evenstar*

drift aft towards the runabout's bows, dropping the bowline in the end of the line Judy had given him over the cleat on the foredeck. 'Right then,' he told me, 'carry on. I reckon with the ebb pushing you to the south you can fetch Barn Pool with the wind on the beam, and we should be able to drag this thing with us. I'll just keep the end of the towing warp in my hand, and sit here on the centreboard case, which'll make her easier to handle.'

Evenstar had started to pay off to starboard. I gave her a helping hand by asking Carol to back the jib to port. 'Let draw,' I called, and the lugger gathered way towards the old fort on the Cornwall side. The line of the tow ran comfortably over the weather quarter, and as he had said, once we were under way, Uncle Jim had no trouble holding it. Within a minute we were out of the middle of the channel, and well clear of the warships' route by the time they started to pass astern.

'What a fun-filled day this is turning out to be,' chuckled Uncle Jim. 'Look at them on the bridge of the leading sweeper, all terribly amused by this little motor boat being towed out of the way by a little sailing boat. I bet they haven't even noticed we've got an ensign let alone expect us to dip it. Judy, you're nearest, perhaps you'd pay our respects to the Royal Navy.'

Judy dipped the ensign from the top of the mizzen.

'Wrong, Jim,' laughed Christine, as the leading sweeper promptly returned the salute.

'Must be someone on the ball there. Pass the binoculars, please someone. Yes, that's what's upset our fun. See the sub-lieutenant on the port bridge wing? Michael Carter, one of my many god-sons, who make up for a superfluity of nieces. Not that you pair don't do pretty well, you handle this little old hooker as smartly as any boy would – better than most, in fact. Talking of which, it's about time we did some seamanlike things like getting ready to anchor. Carol, can you get things sorted out forward, please.'

'And while that's happening,' said Judy, 'perhaps you'd explain what's going on. That was a master stroke wrapping a poly bag round that odious poseur's prop, but why haven't we left him to stew in the middle of the channel, drifting hopelessly out to sea. That would teach him a lesson.'

'Judy, Judy, basking in warm feelings of moral rectitude is a luxury one should only indulge in when you know there will not be a penalty. At sea you never know when you, or indeed someone else, will need a hand. Sure he needs to be taught a lesson, but I have education in mind rather more than I think you do. Besides, I'd like my spinner back.'

'Anchor's ready to go,' sang out Carol.

Uncle Jim asked how I thought we should handle the manoeuvre, which made me feel a bit better; perhaps I wasn't in complete disgrace, never to be allowed in charge again. I thought hard.

'Well, judging by the boats already anchored in the pool, the tide is strong enough to counteract the wind, so we can run down to the anchorage under jib, furl it, and when we've stopped and started to drift back, let the pick go.'

'Good,' said Uncle Jim, 'and the centreplate?'

'Down, to increase the effect of the tide on the hull.'

'Perfect.' Praise indeed. 'Quite what will happen to sunshine astern of us I'm not entirely sure. He may be wind rode, in which case he'll end up alongside, bows to stern, which'll be no bad thing. Or he'll lie astern, in which case we'll have to pull him alongside – again, no bad thing. Right, let's do it. All yours, Sally.'

It was time to take charge again.

'Judy, drop the main. Christine, stow the sail as it comes down, and when you're done, stand by to put a stow on the mizzen. Carol, ready with the anchor. Judy, once you're secured the main halyard, stand by with the jib furling line. Uncle Jim, do you think you could manage the tow, keeping your head clear of the gaff and letting go the jib sheet?'

'Aye aye, ma'am.' He laughed. I was back in favour.

'Aye aye, ma'am,' the others echoed in the sort of exaggerated way they use when they're taking the mickey. I stared them all down, but spoilt it all with a fit of the giggles the others caught.

'Hey, what's going on?' A worried shout from astern reminded us what we were supposed to be about.

'It's OK,' Uncle Jim shouted back. 'We'll be anchored in a jiffy.'

I gave Judy the nod to drop the main and down it came, very smartly, to be swiftly stowed and secured with an elastic cord. Christine clambered around Jim, avoiding stepping over the tow line, unjammed the mizzen, pulled the leach tight down the mast, rolled the sail up and put another bungy cord around it. Judy had the jib furling line in her hand, and Jim the jib sheet. They looked aft.

'OK,' I said, and the jib disappeared, rolled around the forestay. Looking over the side, I saw a piece of weed make its way past the hull, then I looked at the shore, and marked the progress of a rock on the beach past a tree as the tide caught us and we started moving astern. Time to drop the pick. 'Right, Carol, now.'

Carol let the anchor go and surged the line round the cleat in the bows.

'I should say we're in about three metres,' she said.

'There's a mark at ten metres,' said Uncle Jim. 'She'll be OK with that just below the water.'

Evenstar drifted back, and in a minute Carol called out that the ten-metre mark had just run out over the bows. 'That'll do,' I said, real Conrad-like.

'Good, well done,' said Uncle Jim. 'Now let's sort sunshine out, and let me do the talking.' He gave Judy a significant stare while he took in the slack as the red runabout was blown down onto us. He made the end of the line fast on *Evenstar*'s port quarter as Judy pushed the fenders back over the side. The two boats lay side by side, bow to stern.

'Right, let's have a look at your prop,' Uncle Jim said to the young man in the other boat, who was looking very perplexed. 'You tilt it up, and I'll poke around from here.' He leant over the side by *Evenstar*'s shrouds and started pulling the tattered plastic bag away from the propeller. 'Introduce yourselves,' he mumbled. 'I'm Jim Thomson. These are various nieces and pseudo-nieces.'

The young man seemed even more confused. 'David Williams,' he stammered. While we went through our names, and David Williams' attention was diverted, Jim surreptitiously dropped the mackerel spinner into Carol's hand as he disentangled it. Soon he had the mangled remains of his plastic bag free, and offered them to the man.

'Got to keep your eyes peeled in these waters, David. I take it I can call you that?' asked Uncle Jim.

'Well, of course.'

'And talking of keeping a lookout, how come you

didn't see us tack back there? I could have sworn you'd taken in our signal.'

'I had, but I thought you were just going to alter course to go round that little headland. I don't see why you should have wanted to cut straight across the river. Why didn't you go down the other side in the first place?'

'What?' spluttered Judy. 'Don't you know sailing boats can't sail straight into the wind? Don't you think we'd have done that if we could.'

'Steady, girl,' said Uncle Jim. 'I think it's quite clear that David here knew nothing of the sort. You don't sail yourself?' He turned to David.

'No, I've just moved down here from Wales. I've not had a boat before – it all looked rather simple. Now that you mention it, I suppose you can't expect a sailing boat to go straight into the wind – it's always been a mystery to me how they can do anything other than just go straight down wind anyway.'

'Just as I thought,' said Uncle Jim. 'I knew you didn't look like a villain, even if you did behave a bit like one.' Although Uncle Jim always advised us all not to believe the worst until it was proved, this was the first time I'd seen him put the principle into practice.

'Well, I thought you'd deliberately cut me up.'

'Quite so, a forgivable error, even if your reactions were slightly less so. However, we must do something about curing your ignorance. Leave your boat on our anchor here and come for a sail – unless you've got anything more pressing.'

He made it sound as if nothing could be more pressing. This was a surprising turn of events, but not an unpleasant one. Now that he had shrunk from being road hog and veritable ogre, David Williams turned out to be a quietly spoken young Welshman, medium height, medium build, medium brown hair, but nice eyes, and he was beginning to smile, which was attractive.

'We'll leave your engine up – don't want you riding over the cable and cutting it. Carol, can you transfer the anchor line onto that cleat on his bows, please? Right, David, hop over here, and sit down there on the starboard side, opposite Sally. Port and starboard mean the same to you as it does to us?'

'Oh yes, when I decided to buy the boat I had "Port" in red letters on my left thumb, and "Star" in green on my right. Amused the others in the office, but I do know the difference.'

'Must be odd having to learn that as an adult,' Carol commented. 'Sally and I have been sailing with Uncle Jim for so long, I can't remember not knowing the difference.' My cousin can be such a creep at times.

'I can,' chimed in Christine, 'because Judy and I only started a couple of years ago when we first came on holiday with you. Could anyone forget sailing down here chanting "There's a little red port left in the bottle" at the top of our voices?'

'I bet the good people of Torpoint haven't forgotten either – half past six on a Sunday morning was probably not too popular,' remarked Uncle Jim. 'Right, enough of salty reminiscences. Ready to go boating? David, would you like to take the tiller, please? That's that piece of wood in front of you. Judy, jib sheets, Sally, ready with the mizzen, and Christine and Carol the main. I'll let the jib furling line go.' He did, and gave David's boat a push away. As Judy sheeted home the port jib, *Evenstar* gathered way.

'Push the tiller away from you just a bit, David. You'll see that the boat turns to starboard. Mizzen please, Sally.' I freed the small brown sail from its tie and it blew out to port, and then drew as I sheeted it home. 'That's enough, David. Now just keep her heading towards that castle on the Hoe. Tiller to port and she goes to starboard, and vice versa, quite simple really. Don't worry about the rest of the chaos on board, it's just those two girls getting the main up. OK, up she goes.'

Carol pulled on the halyard as Christine ensured the sail caught on nothing on the way up, freed the mainsheets from the tiller, oars and other obstructions, then waited to sheet in while Carol made the halyard fast.

'That'll teach you to let the downhaul off first,' Uncle Jim commented as she had to slacken it off, re-tighten the halyard, and then make the main luff tight again. Carol stuck her tongue out at him. 'Mutinous bunch, and you see what I meant about chaos, David. However, now that Christine has brought order to the natural state of things by getting that mainsheet in, you now see us bowling nicely along on a reach. The wind is more or less coming straight on to the side of the boat, and the sails are about halfway out.'

Evenstar heeled to port, the bow wave made an audible gurgle, and everyone looked very content, except for David. 'Is it supposed to be pulling like this?' he asked. 'I thought I'd got the hang of going in a straight line, but your boat appears to want to go somewhere else.'

'Not surprising, with the great weight we've got to port,' said Judy. 'Perhaps one of you lumps could sit up here and give the poor man a chance.'

'That's very charitable of you, Judy,' Uncle Jim replied. 'I'll come and sit between you, and try and take charge of this anarchy, and explain some of the complexities of this process to young David. See that massive wall on top of the hill over there?' He pointed away to starboard past Drake's Island. When David nodded, he continued, 'Now aim for a point just to the left of it.'

'Right, push the tiller away from me?' David asked, correctly, 'and there we are, whoops!'

As *Evenstar* luffed and the wind was spilled from the sails, the additional weight on the starboard side heeled her that way, and she nearly stopped.

Uncle Jim moved onto the centreboard case, and she came more upright.

'Now, I'm sure you can see that this state of affairs is far from ideal – the boat's practically stopped, you're finding it almost impossible to steer, and it looks horrible.' He got us to sheet the sails in. They stopped flogging, and took up their proper curves. Jim moved to the seat between Judy and David as *Evenstar* again heeled to port and picked up speed.

'Everyone point to where they think the wind's coming from,' Uncle Jim asked us. 'Excellent,' he commented as we all pointed towards the Breakwater Fort.

'David, do you see that as we have altered course more towards where the wind's blowing from, we had to pull the sails in more to keep them working? And would you agree that we couldn't practically pull them in any more?'

'Yes, I see that. Am I still going in the right direction?'

'That's fine, but now come further round to starboard and head for the end of the breakwater.'

David pushed the tiller away from him and *Evenstar* rounded up, the sails flapping, and Uncle Jim moved again to the centreboard case.

'We've stopped.' David moved the tiller to and fro with no effect.

'You're right. And in a second we'll start going backwards. Then we can sort ourselves out and I'll explain. 'Carol, you're nearest, could you push the jib out to port? David, pull the tiller towards you a bit ... that'll do ... just hold it there.'

With the jib aback pushing the bows round to starboard, *Evenstar* turned as she gathered way aft. Uncle Jim got David to shift to the other side; the rest of us stayed put. 'Tiller in the middle now,' he told David. 'Let draw, Carol.'

Carol let the jib fly round to the other side of the mast, and pulled on the other sheet. For a few seconds *Evenstar* wallowed, although the sails were full, before she started to heel to starboard and move again.

Uncle Jim told David to keep her going as she was, picking a rock or a tree, and settle down heading for it while he collected his bearings. Then he asked him where the wind was coming from.

David raised his left arm and pointed towards the breakwater, saying that he didn't think he'd have much trouble with that. It turned out that he's a keen fisherman and wind direction can be quite important there too. You learn something new every day.

'Well, that's half the battle won,' Uncle Jim said. He could remember people still not grasping that after three days when he was teaching sailing for money as a young man. Judy had the decency to blush; it had taken her ages to work out windward and leeward.

Uncle Jim was really stuck in the teaching groove now. 'What do you think will happen if you were to come more to port?'

'Judging by what happened just now, we'll stop. Do you want me to prove it?' David replied.

'Quick, isn't he?' was Carol's comment. 'Judy didn't get there that fast.'

'Phoo,' replied Judy – as I said, she had been a slow beginner.

'Ignore them,' commanded Uncle Jim. 'But yes, only instead of letting the boat stop when you come to port, come back to starboard as you feel her slow, and keep her going just to starboard of where she feels sluggish. That's right, that's pretty good. See how the front edge of the jib starts to lift as you come to the wind? Sail her so that's not quite happening, if you follow me.'

'Yes, got that. Not easy though, is it.'

'Nor's anything worth doing, but you're making a good go of it.'

'I think he deserves a chocolate biscuit,' announced Carol. 'In fact I think we all deserve a chocolate biscuit.'

'In a minute.' Uncle Jim raised his finger. 'This tape isn't finished yet, and if I get interrupted I could miss something vital.' He might feel he had to start all over again, too. 'Still concentrating, David? Good. We've established we can't steer any more to port now, and before we did that business with the flapping sails back there, we had established that we couldn't sail any more to starboard. Do you see where we were heading before the business with the flapping sails? That's called tacking, by the way – a much shorter and handier expression. It's up there on the port beam, right? So we've done a right angle turn, and if you look down there, around the back of the big sail here, you will see your boat, dead down wind. What we have done is to move towards where the wind is blowing from by doing a zig one way then a zag the other. See?'

David did indeed, and now he saw exactly why we did what we did back at Devil's Point. He was pretty mortified. 'What an idiot you must have thought me. I'd really better not go out again on my own until I know more about what's going on.'

'If you've grasped all that, you really do deserve a chocolate biscuit.' Real congratulations from Uncle Jim, that is. Carol handed them round. Then Christine took the helm to get us back to David's little red boat. Uncle Jim reckoned he'd had enough instruction for the time being.

Christine remarked that the tide had turned.

'You're right,' replied Carol. 'There might be some mackerel about, or do you reckon it's too early?'

David was quite interested in that and wanted to know what the tide had to do with it. He'd bought some books on sea fishing but hadn't got round to reading them yet.

'You do sometimes get them coming into the river on the flood,' Uncle Jim told him. 'And whether they are or aren't today, we won't catch any without a hook in the water. You still got that spinner, Carol?' Uncle Jim looked slightly embarrassed when he mentioned it, but Carol produced it without a word, and re-attached it to the end of the line that had been stowed under the seat.

'Can I tie that for you?' David asked.

'No, I can manage perfectly well, thank you,' Carol replied, frightfully put out.

David was sensible enough to take the hint. 'I

suppose you can. You all seem terribly competent in a boat. May I see the rig? I've read a bit about it, but never actually seen one.'

'Sure.' Carol passed it across.

'This is just a very simple and small line that I keep handy,' explained Uncle Jim. 'It's only about twenty metres, so it's quick to get in and out. There's only a single hook spinner, which again makes for ease and speed, and the weight is just a short length of lead pipe so I won't feel too broken-hearted if it snags the bottom and the whole lot breaks off.'

'I see. Pretty strong line though,' David observed, feeling the orange courlene line. 'Doesn't give the fish much of a chance, does it?'

'We don't do it to give the fish a chance,' retorted Carol – David was not making a big hit, I could see. 'The aim is to catch them and eat them. Come on, let's get it over, there are some terns congregating over there to starboard.'

'I see them,' said Christine. 'Stand by to gybe. Best someone gets that plate up. Come along Uncle Jim, you're nearest. Watch your heads.' Bossiness is tolerated when we're after mackerel.

She grasped the mainsheet in a bundle and flicked it over her head as she pulled the tiller towards her. Judy let the starboard jib sheet go. 'Grab that port jib sheet, David,' she shouted as the sail started to flap.

'I'd love to, if someone would point it out. Is this it?'

'Got it in one, young man,' said Uncle Jim. 'We'll make a sailor of you yet, and best you learn fast, this lot are not patient of error if there are mackerel about.'

'There's lots of them now,' shrieked Carol. 'The line's out. Come on, let's get amongst them!'

'I'm doing my best,' Christine replied. 'Let that jib out a bit, David. Uncle Jim, can you look after the mizzen? I can do the main. That's better, isn't it?'

'Quite complicated, this sailing business,' observed David. 'Have I got this right? Not only can I not see the sail this bit of rope's attached to, but I'm not sure what it's supposed to look like anyway.'

'It's fine like that, David,' said Uncle Jim, 'and don't pay too much attention, we're going quite fast enough. That little weight is not enough for any real speed – we'd have the spinner scuttling along on the surface. But for future reference, you need to have the sail as far out as it takes for the front edge not to lift as the wind gets the other side of it. Do you follow? Try it and see.'

David looked under the main at the jib and fiddled with the sheet for a moment. 'Yes, I see what you mean, and it really makes a difference, does it?'

'Too right, sailor,' Judy replied, 'but once we get stuck into a shoal of mackerel, niceties like that tend to get forgotten. Yes, there they are!'

Ahead of us the water boiled, and with a little imagination it was possible to see the mottled green backs of the mackerel porpoising as they chased the small fry to the surface. In seconds, *Evenstar* had passed through the disturbed patch of water, and all eyes looked aft at the line Carol was holding.

She had one on the line.

Jim called for the poly bag – he didn't want fish scales all over his boat.

'But it's gone…' said Judy, dismayed, but she got no further, as Carol interrupted her with a sharp nudge in the ribs.

'It's in the locker underneath you,' she said. 'I put a spare there this morning.' The stress on 'spare' would have been missed by anyone not aware of what had happened to the original plastic carrier bag. Uncle Jim gave her a grateful look.

She hauled the line in, and Judy held open the bag, into which the fish was lowered tail first. She grasped it through the bag, and removed the hook, which she let fall over the side so that Carol could let it out again. In seconds, the operation was repeated, and then again.

'That's pretty efficient,' commented David, 'although hardly sporting, I bet they'd give a good account of themselves on a fly rod. I must try it.'

'Not so easy on a sailing boat,' Uncle Jim said. 'Not that you should listen to me, though. I know nothing about fly fishing other than you have to wave the rod about and catch trees. Perhaps with the main out of the way you'd have room to do that. Should be possible in your boat.'

'Once I know how to handle it properly without being a danger to everyone else, you mean.'

Uncle Jim asked him where he kept it.

'Up the river, just before the big bridge with the funny arches, on the port side going up river, opposite a little creek. Saltash, the town's called. Do you know where I mean? The mooring belongs to a friend who's gone sailing around the Mediterranean for the summer. I'll have to put it in and out on the trailer when he gets back.'

'Nice friend to have,' Judy said enviously. 'I'd love to go sailing somewhere it's always warm. Not that this isn't a lot of fun, and I suppose the changeability of the weather makes for some excitement. And of course, you can't beat a good sail and catching mackerel.' She let another fish drop into the bag and removed the hook. 'That's six,' she counted.

'Enough for one each,' said Christine. 'Let's go round again. Stand by to gybe. You'll have to let that rope go, David, when I say, and watch your head on this block – it might flog a bit. Everyone ready? Good. Here we go. Let it go now, David, Judy will pull it in on the other side. Gybe ho.' Again she flicked the mainsheets across the boat.

'This is a bit like that other business – tacking, did you call it? Only you're turning away from the wind instead of towards it,' David commented.

'Yes, absolutely right,' I said – anyone who learned that fast deserves all the encouragement he can get. 'And the sails go from all the way out on one side to all the way out on the other, instead of all the way in to all the way in.' That was just to show Uncle Jim that I knew his lines. I got a grunt and raised eyebrow in the way of congratulation.

'Got that, it's beginning to make sense now. We've zigzagged downwind, and I see my boat is now ahead.'

Judy pointed out that we hadn't got one mackerel each. 'What about David?' she asked. 'Can you use any?' Now that he'd been proved to be OK, he was clearly due the same consideration she showed the rest of the world. David was sure his landlady could cook some.

'Right you are, one for you, one for your landlady. Any more?' Carol was just after slaughtering more mackerel.

'Her husband is there too, of course. I'm in digs until I find a flat.'

'Three more and then we stop. Do you think we've got time, Uncle Jim?' Carol asked.

'OK, we have to make one more pass through anyway, and then you can drop David and me on his boat – would you like me to come back with you?' Uncle Jim asked David. 'I can fill you in a bit more on rule of the road and customs and manners at sea and all that.'

'Yes please,' David nodded enthusiastically. 'But what will the girls do?'

'They can manage to get back to Saltash on their own. My mooring's only a mile or so up the Lynher from you. They can pick me up, it's not much of a detour. You ladies happy with that?'

Were we ever? The chorus of assent was quickly replaced by more excitement as Carol started pulling in mackerel again. The required three soon joined the others in the plastic bag. Carol stowed it in the locker under the bench seat with the fishing line which she had recovered.

'Now then, Christine. What do you think of the approach to David's boat?' Uncle Jim asked.

I didn't really mind him asking Christine. I was pretty sure he'd leave me in charge, and it does no harm having a crew that understands all the problems. Besides, I was fairly certain I knew the answer, and less sure that Christine would get it. I know, I'm a show-off.

'I'll round up head to wind and let the wind and tide stop her as we get alongside, then you can hop off,' she said.

'Any contrary views?' Uncle Jim looked at us.

'Yes,' I said. I had been looking closely at the anchorage. 'Most of the boats are lying with their bows north; I bet there's an eddy in the bay, and there'll be practically no wind. So we should run down on the jib and let the tide do the stopping.'

'Well spotted' – praise indeed from Uncle Jim – 'or have you been in there before on the early flood? I can't remember. But it doesn't matter, you're dead right. Do you see now, Christine? Your answer was a good commonsense one but, unfortunately, wrong.'

'Yes, never too old to learn.'

'Even at the ripe old age of fifteen and half,' Judy teased.

'Sally,' said Uncle Jim, 'I'm leaving you in charge. Not that I'm not sure that you're all capable, but in a boat you have to have someone responsible for final decisions. OK?' We all nodded.

'It's a very straightforward trip; you've done it lots of times with me. The wind and tide are with you, so you should be quite quick – but watch out for losing steerage way. Don't go too close to the warships, you'll have the Ministry of Defence Police boats chasing you away. Think you can find David's mooring OK?'

I thought it would be no problem, with that bright red hull she ought to stand out very well.

'Good. Now we're nearly there. As you said, Sally, there's not a lot of wind here, so we won't bother with dropping the main. Doing a loose stow up against the mast will do for that and the mizzen, and just hold onto them. The jib you can furl in the normal way if we need to get rid of more sail. David and I will step off as you go past. If we're going too fast we can always go round again, and stream the bucket over the side to slow down. Then once we've got the anchor up, you heave to, we'll come alongside you and pass it back. Everyone know what's going on? Right, let's do it.'

'What about fenders?' queried Judy.

I told her not to bother. 'Even though we'll be

stopped on the ground, we'll be moving and Christine'll have steerage way on so she can keep clear. Besides, it's so calm, Uncle Jim can push off with his foot.' Then I remembered that Uncle Jim was still in charge, and apologised, 'I don't have the ship yet, do I?'

'Saucy madam.' He laughed. 'But you're dead right. If Christine's up to it, that is.'

'Of course I am.'

The evolution went just as we had said it should. With loosely furled sails *Evenstar* stopped in the tide alongside David's boat, allowing the two men to step off without losing way through the water. Christine was able to steer all the time and keep the boats apart – the fenders were not needed.

'Now you have the ship,' said Uncle Jim as he stepped across.

'I have the ship,' I replied.

'What's that all about?' I heard David ask once they were on his boat.

'Very naval custom,' Uncle Jim replied. 'Not really necessary in small boats, but it never hurts to make sure everyone knows who's in charge. Very competent is our Sally, but given their own way, the others would tend to run the boat by committee.'

Judy heard him and shouted at him.

I took charge. 'And he's dead right, so stow the gab, as we bucko down-easter mates say, and clap onto them sheets there. We'll work our way out of this eddy and back into the tide once we've transferred the anchor.' It may not have been the fastest way home, but I didn't fancy doing it in the middle of the narrows with the tide boring in.

The others looked at each other and nodded. 'Let it be recorded in the minutes that the committee endorsed the Captain's decision,' said Carol. An unruly bunch, but good to have around.

Once we'd settled down, I told Judy to back the jib and Christine to let the main right out. We left the mizzen as it was. With the helm down, *Evenstar* practically stopped, gently luffing then falling back off the wind. The slight wake stretched away from the starboard quarter as she drifted downwind.

Uncle Jim and David had by now recovered *Evenstar*'s anchor and were approaching us from up-wind. David sat on the tiny foredeck as Uncle Jim gently brought the bows almost against *Evenstar*'s starboard side. Then he leant over to pass the anchor and line.

'I thought it better he drove,' he said with a smile, 'then if anything goes wrong and you get sunk, it's not my fault. Though it seems unlikely – he seems to know a lot about boats.'

'Dead right,' Judy said. 'Gosh, we remember when –'

'Have you done, David?' interrupted Uncle Jim. 'Don't let those girls start gassing. I can't keep the boat in this position for ever.'

David laughed, shrugged his shoulders, and gave Uncle Jim a thumbs-up signal through the windscreen as he left the foredeck for the cockpit aft. Uncle Jim gave a burst astern and we separated without ever having touched. Once they were at a safe distance the two men changed places. David engaged forward gear and steered past us. They waved, and I heard Uncle Jim saying, 'Now, at sea we drive on the right, not on the left, and the rules for keeping out of the way are much more complicated,' before they were out of earshot.

'An hour's worth of rule of the road coming up for Mr Williams,' my cousin said with a laugh.

'I hope he realises his luck,' said Judy. 'Think of

the damage he could have caused if your uncle hadn't taken charge of him.'

'I rather liked him,' Christine commented. 'Apart from that burst of temper when we first crossed paths, he seems, well, innocent. Do you think he's likely to be around for the summer?'

'I should think so,' said Carol. 'He said he was looking for a flat.'

'And we're likely to be here still if we don't get a move on,' I reminded them, and set Judy to stowing the anchor and line. Then Christine let the mizzen fly and pulled the helm up. Once *Evenstar* was pointing towards Devil's Point, Carol let the jib draw, and I pulled the plate up. When we had a decent amount of way on, Christine gybed and we cracked on up the Hamoaze. With the early flood and the wind over the quarter we really sped over the ground.

We had no problem finding them at Saltash. Not only was the red hull conspic, but they were the only ones practising picking up a mooring. Round and round they went.

'Your uncle's giving quite a demonstration there,' Judy remarked. 'I wonder what sort of a hash David'll make of it?'

She really had to eat her words and change her opinions of David when we came closer and found he had been driving all the time.

Once back on *Evenstar*, Uncle Jim explained that he had shown him a couple of times, and he'd picked it up straight away. Indeed, he seemed to have been quite impressed with David on their trip up river. He listened – one of Uncle Jim's favourite traits in someone else – and only needed to be told something once. Apparently David had gone into partnership with a couple of guys he'd known at university and had started Graphics South West, which Uncle Jim reckoned was just the firm to produce a job he was working on. He broke off from explaining further.

'I'm afraid we're going to have to put the chug on.' David's mooring off Saltash was above the Lynher, which was where we had to go, so we were flogging against both wind and tide with little success. 'Once past Wearde Quay we should be OK. Furl the jib please, Carol,' he said as the evening quiet was shattered by the outboard's roar. Then he apologised for taking over without referring to me – one of the many things we like about him is the way he treats us as people not children. Conversation was not really on with the Johnson rattling away on the stern, but once we could sail again, the jib was unfurled and the engine stopped and tilted back up.

'Who has the ship?' I wanted to know.

'How about Judy picking up the mooring?' Uncle Jim suggested. 'I'm sure they've all had quite enough of you being in charge this afternoon.' Me!

'OK,' said Judy. 'Give us the helm.'

We changed places. We had been sitting on opposite sides, and Judy's a bit heavier than me – well, quite a lot really – so *Evenstar* heeled to windward, and in the failing breeze practically stopped. As fairly often happens on this junction of the two rivers, the wind that had been blowing from the south up the Tamar was blowing from the west here, down the Lynher. Fortunately we had the tide with us, or we'd have stopped dead, with the mooring in sight, and perilously close to supper time. But before even Carol had a chance to complain about the risk of missing a meal, Judy took charge.

'Come on, Jim,' she said. 'We can't have two lumps

on this side in this wind, and you know I'd rather sit to windward to steer. So how about you shift?'

Unoffended, he moved onto the centreboard case. *Evenstar* heeled to leeward, the sails fell into their proper shape and we started to gather way again.

Uncle Jim was just about to tell us what he planned to do with David when Christine interrupted. 'Watch this.' She nodded in the direction of the Tamar, astern. 'I predict some entertainment.'

On our lee quarter, on a parallel course and heading towards the last of the moorings off Wearde Quay, was a rather fine half decked keelboat – similar to a Dragon, or Sunbeam, but not quite the same.

'That's Pascoe. He owns, or rather half owns, the small yard we've just passed there – Pascoe and Brothers. I was just about to tell you about them. They're going to start doing customised high-class, craftsman finishing jobs on a standard thirty-five-foot hull. A firm in the Midland makes the hulls, and Pascoe and Brothers down here, and another firm on the Clyde, do all the tiddlying up. I'm doing the words for the brochure for P and B, and I need someone to do the pictures, artwork and layout. David's bunch should be just right, and it'll keep Mr Brothers happy – although he's not Cornish, he's dead keen on supporting local business.' He turned his attention to the sloop. 'Super little boat that, used to be a fleet of them around here, but only a few left now. Belongs to Pascoe and wasted on him.' Uncle Jim had never liked or trusted Pascoe. His instincts were right but we didn't know that at the time.

'I bet he's going to pick up that last mooring,' Christine went on. 'He was there this morning, lying bows west, and he looks as if he's going to try to get back on the same way.'

'Right,' said Judy, who had stopped concentrating on her own helming. 'Only he won't stop, because he's got the tide under him. I wonder if his crew's strong enough to hold it.'

'Bet he falls in,' said Carol, who clearly disliked the poor anonymous crewman, probably only because he was in a boat with someone Uncle Jim couldn't stand – we're a fairly loyal lot.

I decided to stick my neck out. 'I'll tell you what's going to happen. He'll luff, and the crew will grab the buoy, and she'll stop, but by then the crew will be wrapped round the shrouds and unable to get the line on the cleat. Once she's stopped, the tide will be sloshing up the stern – she'll be making a sternboard – it'll grip the rudder and flick it round, which'll tear the tiller out of Pascoe's hand, then she'll start to swing head to tide, gybing on the way. With all that sail, she'll make way against the tide, and the poor old crew, having been practically rolled out off the deck by the gybe, will then fall in, leaving po-face charging down the river out of control.' I didn't like him either.

To my lasting delight, a moment to cherish for ever – after all, the gift of prophecy is rarely given – it happened just like that, only even better. The tiller caught Pascoe behind the knees, tumbling him into the bottom of the boat. He scrambled up just in time to be thumped on the shoulders by the boom. By the time he came back into sight he was alone; his crew, evidently female from her voice, was clinging to the buoy and calling in very unladylike language for him to come back.

'Well.' Judy turned to Uncle Jim. 'That was fun,

but I suppose we should go leaping to the rescue.'

'Tricky,' Uncle Jim thought. 'We'll go through the motions, but sure as eggs we won't be welcomed, at least by Pascoe, so just make sure we don't get there before him.'

Gently, Judy gybed *Evenstar* round, and we stemmed the tide, making very little way towards the moored crewperson. Pascoe had sorted himself out and tacked up almost to where we were, then luffed to drop his main.

'Can we help?' Uncle Jim yelled out.

'No, you damn well can't. Push off and get out of my way. Can't you see I'm on my own with that damn fool woman falling out of the boat? She can damn well sit there until I get back to her. Go on. Shove off.' Not a particularly pleasant reply, but then he can't have been a very pleasant person. If Judy had not been convinced before, she was now – she was spluttering she was so cross – though she did manage a perfectly good gybe to get us back on track up the Lynher.

'What an odious man! I hope she pushes him in. How does he get anyone to sail with him?' and so on.

'Because his boat is a perfect gem, and he's single and absolutely loaded, though where it comes from I have no idea, that yard can hardly be much of a money spinner. Still, his partner's OK, a bit pompous, but his heart's in the right place. Enough for today, I think. Time to get home.'

Uncle Jim asked me to start the outboard. Fortunately, you never needed to pump the squidgy thing on the petrol line to prime it – it's an awful sweat getting the after hatch off with all the feet and sheets and things in the way – and as usual it started on the second pull. One of the nice things about sailing with the same people all the time is that everyone knows what needs to be done and just gets on with it. Carol furled the jib and started putting the cover on. Jim and Christine took the main down and stowed it, lashing it out of the way up the mast, and I rolled the mizzen round the mast and put the cover on that. By the time we reached the mooring *Evenstar* was secured. It only remained for the last one to go ashore to put the cover over the cockpit for the job to be complete.

2

Next day, Sunday, was a very rare treat. We were let loose on the river on our own. Having been cleared of all blame for getting snarled up with David's boat in the first place, I was put in charge of *Evenstar*. What would I have done if he'd not been there? Uncle Jim had asked. I told him I would have chickened out and gybed round to go under his stern, and he admitted that as he'd said to tack, the whole incident was down to him. Pretty decent really.

Hardly surprisingly, we were terribly excited. Even though we weren't due to set off until late morning, we rose early enough for the forecast, which was for southerlies, with a not particularly active Atlantic depression on its way.

Uncle Jim and Aunt Liz had to go to a staff lunch. They were both contributors to the local freebie paper, the *Saltash Sentinel*, and the editor (who took himself rather seriously) thought it good for team morale for them all to get together for Sunday lunch once a month. Normally Uncle Jim was a reluctant participant, or even a non-attender, but he'd persuaded Andrew Davis that instead of the usual pie and a pint in the Red Lion, they should meet in the Old Mill, a rather up-market restaurant just out of town, the proprietor having been convinced that the *Saltash Sentinel* editorial team would lend tone to the place.

I think the promise of a favourable review and cheap ad space had more to do with it.

Uncle Jim fussed around us like a mother hen, but Aunt Liz shut him up when he asked for the umpteenth time if we understood we weren't to go beyond the breakwater.

'Sally knows what she's doing – and it's not really the first time. She managed perfectly well coming back from Barn Pool yesterday; there really is no difference between sailing from there to here and sailing from here to there and back, is there?'

He had to agree, and at eleven o'clock they waved goodbye to us as we broad reached down the Lynher towards the Tamar. The depression had deepened and was coming a little faster than expected, so we were close hauled with a south westerly force four and a bit once we were in the main river, and we tucked the reef in. The sun was shining, but there were a few high clouds around to hide it from time to time – definitely not a bronzing day.

Our plan, having read what literature was available in the Thomsons' collection of local history books, was to examine the seaward aspect of the fortifications, starting with Kingsand in the west. We could carry the ebb out through the Bridge, then along the coast into Cawsand Bay. Then we would have a run back with the early flood, which would let us go as close in as we liked as far as Fort Picklecombe. The tide would be good to cross the Sound to have a look at Bovisand, returning via the main channel which passes to the east of Drake's Island, which we would then have circumnavigated. The flood would get us home, even if by then the wind had increased and we were just under jib and mizzen.

The plan worked perfectly. We even had time to

rescue Jean-Pierre – which was the event that made that Sunday memorable.

There was about an hour and a half of tide left to ebb when we hit the Narrows; and a couple of knots of stream with us, which promised to make the sea quite lumpy, as we passed through the Bridge, with wind opposing tide, an uneven bottom and, notwithstanding the breakwater, a long fetch to windward. With only slightly mutinous muttering from Carol, we got rid of the main, putting a good tight stow on it and lashing the gaff up against the mast. Without the main, *Evenstar* doesn't sail as close to the wind and I wasn't sure whether we'd weather the western end of the shoal running out from Drake's Island. There was a good chance of a favourable shift closer to the gap, and I wasn't too worried, but I was paying a lot of attention to sailing her to windward well. So it was Judy who first spotted the ketch running in from seaward for the same gap. It was no cause for worry. Drawing so little, we had plenty of room to manoeuvre and I reckoned I could keep well clear of him, even though we were on starboard and he on the port tack and supposed to keep clear of us. We could quite happily cut the corner and go outside the channel marker if necessary.

'I hope he knows what he's doing,' she commented. 'That's a lot of sail to have up running onto a lee shore single-handed.'

'I bet he needs it,' Carol replied. 'It's a Hillyard, I think, or something like it. They're really not at all fast, but very easy to handle. You remember Uncle Jim used to have one, not as big as that though, and reckoned you should never attempt to buck a foul tide in one. He must be in a bit of a hurry when all he's got to do is wait another hour.'

Christine interrupted her. 'No, he's foreign. Look, he's flying a courtesy flag and the yellow Q flag. What do you bet he's French and forgotten the hour change, so he thinks it's low water?'

She was right about him being foreign, but wrong about him making a mistake over the time of the tide. As we discovered later, Jean-Pierre was just being typically foolhardy.

At that point his mizzen sheet parted company from the boom. His bows paid off, and a bigger than average wave caught his stern and he broached, both booms swinging wildly across as he gybed. We saw the helmsman thrown across the cockpit as he failed to duck far enough below the main boom. We could only watch helplessly as the ketch left the channel and piled onto the south-west end of the shoal.

'Isn't there anything we can do?' Christine wanted to know.

'We'd need to get alongside him to get a line on to tow him off,' Carol said.

But I knew that wouldn't work – there was no way *Evenstar*'s little Johnson would be enough to pull a boat that size off. It would take its own engine, and an anchor, and even then the sails would have to come down. I was not at all sure that I fancied putting *Evenstar* alongside the ketch with its sails up; it looked to be prone to gybing as it rolled. If only the skipper was OK – and he was. Even as I was wallowing in indecision, a blond head appeared above the cockpit coaming. The man scurried forward and cast off the jib halyard, and in no time had the sail down and lashed on the rail. The main was more difficult with the wind pressing it against the shrouds, but that came down too.

Perhaps he'd be able to motor off, I hoped, as he

leapt aft to tame the mizzen, which had pushed the stern round so the boat was lying broadside on to the sea, with the bows towards the breakwater. Although the depth was decreasing, it was not doing so quickly, and the ebb was at least pushing him towards deeper water; but the wind was the stronger, setting him further onto the rocks. We saw a cloud of black smoke from his exhaust as he started the engine, and the water boiled under the canoe stern, but he was unable to get her up to windward. He needed an anchor laid out to windward, otherwise he stood a good chance of becoming a complete wreck.

As we passed to windward of him I shouted that we would lay out a kedge, but the men did not seem to understand. 'Idiot, Sally,' said Christine. 'Even if he can hear you over the engine, he's probably not up to concentrating on English with all this going on, and a bash on the head. *Nous posons un ancre,*' she shouted.

She was quite right. I had failed to appreciate the significance of the tricolour at his mizzen mast head. Christine's French may not have been perfect, but it was adequate. We made out *'Merci, vite, vite,'* in the reply.

It was time to take charge. Judy dragged the anchor out of the stern locker, and an enormous warp which Uncle Jim can only have kept there for eventualities such as this. Carol, as the expert, readied the heaving line. Christine tied two fenders onto the end of the warp. By the time all this was done, the ketch was about 150 metres astern and it was time to tack. I wanted to work back to a position about 50 metres upwind of him, drop the pick, run down towards him paying out the warp, then gybe and luff back onto a southerly heading at the same time as Carol threw the heaving line to him. The heaving line was attached to the fenders on the end of the main warp, so even if it all went wrong we could at least pick them up and have another go.

And it all went correctly, thankfully, even though it was quite a heart-stopping manoeuvre. Crashing to windward, we knew there was something of a sea running, but I had expected it to seem a lot less once we'd turned downwind.

The rope fairly whipped through the crutch on the port side and over the transom – it was a good thing Judy had done such an efficient job of laying it out; a snag could have been disastrous. I had judged the distance well enough, there was still 20 metres left in the boat as Carol, with a beautiful left-handed throw dropped the monkey's fist on the heaving line between the ketch's masts. We were about 10 metres off (it must have been, but it looked a lot less at the time) as I pushed the tiller to port and hardened the mizzen sheet. Someone did the same to the jib – I'd forgotten to tell anyone, but it didn't matter, we were really working well together. There was a nasty moment when it looked like the anchor line might snag on the bumkin, but as *Evenstar* climbed up a wave, it slipped free.

Our friend took the heaving line forward, then pulled the fenders with the end of the main warp attached inboard. There was indeed enough slack for him to be able to put it on his anchor winch. He pulled it tight then got to work with the handle. The heavy nylon line lifted clear of the water, drips flying off as it came under strain. The anchor seemed to be holding, as it ought to have done; we have often kidded Uncle Jim about the outsize gear he kept on the lugger. He'd now got enough spare line to bring it back to his jib sheet winch where he could wind and work the engine controls.

By then we were hove to on port tack more or less due south of him. Had we been in time, or did he not have enough water to get off? The prop thrashed the water to foam and the anchor line was bar taut. But slowly his bows came up into the wind, and the engine was able to push him towards deeper water. There were a couple of shudders as she bounced, then she was definitely off. Once clear, the man cut the engine and lay back on our anchor while he disappeared below.

'Obviously not a complete idiot,' was Judy's comment. 'Probably very sensible to have a look for the water coming in. He'll be lucky to have got away with that.'

We were within shouting distance when the man reappeared. 'Are you OK?' I called out.

'*Ça va*? You twit,' hissed Christine. 'Have you forgotten he's a Frog?'

Fortunately, OK is international, and the man was now able to think a bit more clearly.

'Yes, thank you. Old Hillyard knew how to make strong boats.'

'See, told you it was a Hillyard,' said Carol, who'd have been prepared to sit there and gossip about old boats if I'd not shut her up.

'Just throw the line over the side when you're ready to go,' I told him. 'We made it so it would float. We can pick it up, there's plenty of water there for us.'

He was very complimentary about our seamanship, and said that as he was going up to Saltash, he would see us later to say thanks. He was also very dishy, which is possibly why even Judy did not suggest afterwards that we ought to have got him to sign a salvage agreement before we went to work.

Collecting the anchor went more easily than I'd feared – it was just hard work. We luffed onto the fenders bobbing in the waves, brought the warp over the bow fairlead and furled the jib. The mizzen kept *Evenstar* head to wind, and we were all able to lay on the cable and haul it in. The bows buried once as we came up to the anchor, but the boat's buoyancy did the hard work for us and broke the anchor free. Then it was a simple task to unfurl and back the jib to get her paying off to port; we stowed all the gear while we were hove to, then got going again.

So we were very smug and self-satisfied as we completed most of the rest of what we had set out to do. It had become rather bouncy by the time we reached Fort Picklecombe, so we went no further that way. But we had a cracking good sail across the Sound, particularly once in the calmer water inside the breakwater (for which even Judy agreed we should be grateful to the Victorians), over to Fort Bovisand, then across Jennycliff Bay. As the tide had started to flood, we reckoned it safe to have a close look at Drake's Island and a good poke around the rocks on the lee side before pushing on home up the river.

We had done very little work while we were out. Judy had made a couple of quick sketches, and we took a few photos, but it had been blowing a bit and the spray had not helped. If anything, the trip had only showed us just how ignorant we were of the history of the river, which Carol and I thought we knew quite well. Dank though it may have seemed, we were going to have to spend time in the library.

Uncle Jim had warned us as much the previous day, but we'd scoffed. None of us wanted to produce a bad project. Apart from the fact that we took a certain pride in our work, there was the possibility that the school would no longer look favourably on our all going on holiday together if they thought it was interfering with work. Parental circumstances were unlikely to change for a year or two for any of us, and holidays in Saltash were the best substitute. Besides, we didn't want to let Uncle Jim down. He had persuaded Miss Welford that we should be allowed to collaborate by assuring her that he would supervise us. By what he described as judicious misinformation, he had let her form the opinion that he was a respectable writer, of whom she should have heard, and could certainly be trusted with such a task.

Although he and Aunt Liz are both writers, he's not really serious. I've already mentioned the brochure he was doing for Pascoe and Brothers. His main work is writing travel brochures – after giving up being a navigator in the Navy he had run his own travel agency, which he had sold, very profitably, a few years later. Although by then he didn't need to work, he kept on with that part of the job, freelance, for fun. We'd thought it must be the perfect job until we discovered he didn't actually go to all the exotic places he described. He might have been once upon a time, but mostly the info came from the library, the consulate and the travel firms – a bit of a fraud really. It meant he was incredibly well read though, and had an amazing web of contacts everywhere.

He was sure, we thought, to like Christine's idea, which she had when passing the site of the old Royal Western Yacht Club. This was building the project around a journey up the Tamar in a yacht in 1900, with an elder statesman of Plymouth. Uncle Jim had been a member of the Royal Western for years, and we were sure he could help with finding a fictitious, if not real, character of the right age and background into whose mouth we could put all that we might find out about the 60 years in question.

These discussions lasted until we reached the Lynher, where we had to turn left, and as before, harden up to beat the last mile to the Thomsons' mooring, just off their house. The first tack took us towards Pascoe and Brothers' yard, and we were rather surprised to see the French ketch on one of their moorings: they're not the usual place for visitors. It was certainly the same yacht, even though the French flag and yellow Q flag were missing, the Hillyard stern was quite distinctive, and Christine – alone of us, strangely enough – had noted the name: *Ariel*. We passed close enough to hail, but there was no one on board.

We found out why half an hour later, once we'd put *Evenstar* on her mooring and rowed ashore. Our Frenchman was comfortably ensconced in the Thomsons' kitchen drinking tea. His good friend Monsieur Pascoe, he said, had told him where to find the very gallant owner of the little blue boat. Uncle Jim and Aunt Liz, of course, hadn't the faintest idea what he'd been talking about when he'd turned up with bottles of champagne, a whole brie and vast amounts of gratitude. Then he'd told them the story – rather highly coloured, I thought when he told it again – but I was relieved to see that Uncle Jim was impressed and whole-heartedly approved. I was a bit worried that he might have been cross that I'd put *Evenstar* at risk.

The Frenchman's name was Jean-Pierre, and he was a great hit with everyone, kissing all the ladies' hands very Gallicly, and being very enthusiastic about his Hillyard, which made Uncle Jim warm to him. He was going to spend a month or so pottering around Devon and Cornwall, and would see much more of us, and would be *enchanté* if we would honour him by sailing with him sometime – of course we would.

After Jean-Pierre had gone, Uncle Jim made us tell the story again, and I could see that he was a little relieved that our version sounded less sensational than Jean-Pierre's, although he was still impressed. 'It was very well done,' he said. 'To have done it at all is quite an achievement, but to do it without making it into a drama is something else. I'm very proud of you all.' I can still hear him saying it; I was chuffed to bits to get praise like that.

He continued, 'Do you see what I meant before about helping someone out when they're in trouble? In material terms you've not done terribly well. I'm afraid you can't have much more than a half glass of champagne each, but I'm sure you'll make pigs of yourselves on the brie; however, you'll always have the satisfaction of a good bit of seamanship well done.' At times Uncle Jim takes the *in loco parentis* role a bit seriously.

'Don't forget we get a sail in *Ariel*,' Carol butted in.

'Not unchaperoned, you don't,' said Aunt Liz. 'Can't run the risk of you folks being whisked away,' she laughed. 'We'll tell you more over dinner. Now come on.'

She set some of us to work, and some to baths and showers, and in about half an hour we and it were ready.

Over supper, Aunt Liz enlarged on the dangers of us being 'whisked off'. 'Andrew Davis, our editor, has this grandiose thing about us being a real newspaper, and he gave us all a pep talk this morning about not letting our journalistic instincts be blunted by the obduracy of the bureaucrats – or some garbage like that. And, of course, young Jason – he's the one that covers big local weddings, young farmers' meetings, village fetes, that sort of thing – sees himself as an ace reporter just waiting for his big break. Do you girls still read *Superman*? Do you remember, what's-his-name Olsen, Superman's friend, and cub reporter of the *Globe*?'

'*Planet*,' corrected Uncle Jim.

We had seen the film, so we knew who she was talking about.

'Well, Jason's just like him, terribly earnest, and he's convinced he's onto a big story. It seems there has been a spate of disappearances of teenage girls from the South West this summer, and the word from those who know is that they've been grabbed for the white slave trade and whisked off to durance vile in the desert somewhere. The spate, however, turns out to be two in Torquay in March, one from Exeter in June, and another from Torquay last week, and poor Jason was quite put out when we all reckoned they'd probably just run off to London. But you four watch out, we don't want to have to phone your folks to tell them you've been dragged away to some sheik's tent in the desert, or flogged off in the bargain end of the casbah.'

The idea made us laugh too. Carol reckoned she rather fancied lounging around in a harem, nothing to do but eat all day, or maybe stick a diamond in her navel and wobble about a bit. That amused us as well – although she changed her mind when Uncle Jim pointed out she'd have to eat sheep's eyeballs. And that was that – not that we'd think it was funny now – the topic was lost in all the good things to eat.

Aunt Liz is a particularly good cook; she also writes about it. You may have read the stuff she writes for one of the national Sunday papers under her maiden name, Elizabeth Carmichael, on vegetables. We had prised that secret out of her at half term when Judy had complained that, having drawn extensively on one of her articles for a home economics essay on cooking for a vegetarian, she had been accused of plagiarism. Actually she'd copied it practically word for word, but Aunt Liz had laughed, said she was very flattered and told Judy she had her permission to breach her copyright any time she liked. She is also the *Saltash Sentinel* food and wine editor, and does a series on fish cookery under the nom de plume of Pescatore – which increased her standing in Carol's eyes. We do love our bellies, we four.

Dinner that night was quite a gay affair. Uncle Jim let us have a whole glass of Jean-Pierre's champagne, and there were lots of good things to eat, including the brie. Even having to talk about work didn't dampen things that much.

The next day we were to be despatched into Plymouth on the bus to spend the morning in the library. Aunt Liz would meet us for lunch, and bring us back. There might be time for a short sail in the evening if the weather was anything like, and Uncle Jim would give us a run round his computer which we could use for writing up the project. He liked the idea of finding or inventing a Victorian yachting worthy to hang it on, and promised to talk to the yacht club secretary to see if we could have access to the club's annals.

3

The bus trip into Plymouth was dull, enlivened only by a glimpse of the Eddystone as we came down the hill to the library. The wind had gone round to the west and was blowing hard; and even from that distance we could see breaking seas across the Sound; a good day not to be at sea.

We got off at the stop outside the library, entered the double doors and followed the signs up the stairs to the local and naval history and reference sections.

Entering the room labelled 'Local History', we found the librarian at her desk, gumming cuttings from the local paper onto sheets of plain A4. Not at all the aged guardian of sacred texts that we had expected, Mrs Carstairs, as her badge proclaimed, was a slim, dark-haired, elegant woman in her forties, although she made one concession to the classical image with her spectacles perched on the end of her nose, the thin gold chain that stopped them getting lost hanging down her back. Otherwise the room was empty of people.

'Yes?' She looked over her spectacles at us, her eyes resting briefly on each in turn. It was not a welcoming scrutiny; sticking in newspaper cuttings was clearly an urgent and important task.

'Don't forget it's the librarian's job to get books and people together, not keep them apart, but helping people who don't help themselves is most frustrating,' had been Uncle Jim's advice. 'Even if you don't know exactly what you want, make it clear that you have some idea. And relax, be natural, smile – libraries are not holy places.'

'Good morning, Mrs Carstairs, we hope you can help us find some material for our project.' Judy smiled.

'Yes?' Mrs Carstairs continued gluing.

This was not proving quite as painless as hoped. 'We're looking for stuff on the Tamar around the 1890s,' Judy continued.

Mrs Carstairs glanced round the room. The walls were mostly lined with books, except where a number of cabinets of little drawers to hold index cards protruded. A collection of large cabinets stood towards one end, and by craning her neck, Carol could see a number of maps strewn over the top of them. Apart from Mrs Carstairs' desk and filing cabinets, the rest of the furniture consisted of half a dozen tables and chairs.

'Well, this is the library, local history section, so I suppose you have come to the right place. Do you have anything particular in mind?'

Oh dear, I thought, we've lost control of this. Judy should have made it plain that we did have something particular instead of her having to ask.

I decided to take charge. 'We know exactly where we would like to start, please. I'd like to look at the back numbers of the local papers; Judy will start wading through *Kelly's Directories*, if you could show her where they are; and Christine would like to examine any maps you have of the area around those dates. If you can show us how the catalogue is arranged I am sure we can manage. My name's Sally Carson. Hello.'

Mrs Carstairs stood up and smiled, and let her glasses hang down. 'Sally, Christine, Carol and Judy, with quite a tall order. I'm not sure you've split the work quite equitably, but it's a good way to begin. Let me start you with the pictures and the *Kelly's Directories*, they're the easiest. Judy and Carol, I think – was it not? Come this way.'

She made her way around the tables to the far corner by the window, and pointed out a section of shelving full from ceiling to wall with immensely thick, brown leather-bound volumes. 'Those are the *Kelly's*; most years are there from 1860 something to 1930 something. The Devon and Cornwall volumes have Devon at the front, then Cornwall, arranged in alphabetical order of towns, and at the back is a classified list of traders. Quite a mountain to mine, I'm afraid, but there are nuggets of gold in there.

'And now the pictures. These are arranged in these cupboards.' She opened one. 'People, arranged alphabetically by name, along the top. North Devon towns, again alphabetically, here, Cornwall, Devon, Rivers, Churches. Get the picture? Ho, ho. That was a joke. Even librarians have a sense of humour. And feel free to talk if there's no one else here, which will probably be the case.'

'Not quite the dragon I first thought,' Christine whispered to me.

'No, surprisingly cheerful, and on the ball too. Notice how she got all our names first time.'

'And she seems to know about what's in here. Do you think she'd like to move to St Agatha's? She's be an improvement on Smaug or Grendel's mother.' You can see why we were a bit nervous of librarians if the school ones enjoyed nicknames like that.

'Now, Christine. You wanted to look at maps I think.'

'Yes, please.'

'Right, I'll come back to you in a minute, because you'll need a hand, so I'll set up your friend first on the microfiche reader, which is in the reference section just across the passageway here. Have you ever used a fiche reader before?' she asked as I followed her out of the door.

'No. Unless you're at one of the top flight boarding schools, you don't find the latest in modern technology.'

'Don't be deceived by fancy bits of kit. They're only as good as the people that want to use them – if there's no curiosity there in the first place, you might just as well have piles of old newspapers done up with string as catalogued and indexed microfiches.'

She took me into the reference section and gave me a box containing a roll of film. It turned out dead easy to fit into the machine, which looked like a fifties TV set. You start with a picture of the whole double page in print too small to read, but changing the lens zooms in on about half a page, making it legible. Little handles wind the film on or back. 'Are you looking for something definite?'

I told her the project title. 'A journey up the Tamar, Then and Now', and that we were at the very first stages, just picking up background.

'Hoping that serendipity will work, eh? Well, it often does, and the only thing you can guarantee is that you won't find anything if you don't start looking.'

'The only certain thing in fishing is that a hook out of water doesn't catch anything. One of my Uncle Jim's bits of wisdom,' I replied, thinking that he'd quite like Mrs Carstairs.

'Now that you've got it from two sources, you can say that research indicates the conventional wisdom holds that knock and the door may open, don't knock and it won't. Happy? I'll leave you here. And,' she looked round, and dropped her voice, 'they're a stuffy lot in here: talking not encouraged. I've just had a very stern look from a member of the public!' She went back to sort Christine out.

I started wading through the papers. It soon stopped being novel and fun. I'd got the *Western Daily Mercury* and *Western Morning News* for 1890, chosen at random, and dull stuff it is too. At least scholars in another century will have pictures to look at when they scan holograms of the *Saltash Sentinel*, or whatever method they'll be using then. But there were one or two items of interest – shipwrecks, for instance – and I could see it would be a useful source for contemporary quotes. The trouble with that was that you'd need to have an idea of what you were looking for – I couldn't see chance helping much. I was getting experience and practice with the controls, though, and after an hour I could scan a complete edition in a few minutes, focusing on possibly more interesting things; like, for example, the *Western Morning News* of the second of April, which contained an article about a proposal to advertise Plymouth with a fancy book, well mounted, strongly bound and 'to ensure its being placed on the tables of the leading clubs and hotels in this country, on the Continent, in America' etc. An early version of glossy in-flight magazines, I thought, which would be unbelievably useful to us if we could find one. In the next couple of weeks we wasted quite a lot of time failing to do that. Uncle Jim and Mrs Carstairs encouraged us too, and both agreed that it wasn't time wasted if it was a dead end – valuable lesson in life and all that. I found no more of use that day, and when my eyes started to get tired I returned the films and went back to the others.

Mrs Carstairs had been terribly helpful with Christine, digging out all sorts of maps. Nearly all the available table space was overflowing with paper – thin crinkly paper, stiff cartridge paper, tracing paper and cloth, photocopied reproductions.

She said she couldn't guarantee getting the exact year and at the scale we might be after, but there was a good selection there.

Christine had been started off with a one-inch Ordnance Survey map which showed the river, from the 1870s. She'd scored a few points for us by guessing its earliest date. We had noticed '1869' on the end pier of the railway bridge across the Tamar for the first time that morning, but Mrs Carstairs wasn't to know that when Christine had airily announced, 'It must be seventies at the earliest, Brunel's bridge has 1869 in big letters on the end.'

That had helped show that we were serious, and Mrs Carstairs had pulled out one-inch maps, 25,000:1 scale maps (which we were much happier with) and even 2,000:1 maps. Then she had to get on with the paper cuttings, but we were to feel free to ask if we wanted more, and unless she got some stuffy customers, she didn't mind if we talked.

'Is it possible to get copies of these pictures?' Judy was asking as I came in.

Mrs Carstairs told her she could photocopy them in the machine across the hall, twenty pence a sheet, but the quality of reproduction of photographs was not high.

'Thanks,' Judy said. 'It's a shame they haven't dated these pictures. Look at these.' She showed them to us. 'These must be around the right period, but they could be anything from 1860 to 1910. And they are just the sort of thing we need – we could easily take pictures from almost exactly the same positions as these were taken.'

'Where's that one, with them building that bridge?' Carol asked.

Judy turned the card over. ' "Calstock – Construction of the Viaduct",' she read out.

'I can help there,' Christine butted in. 'I've got a one-inch map here of 1899 with no railway bridge, and somewhere here, there's a two and half thou.' She broke off and rummaged through her pile of maps. 'Yes, here it is. Calstock, 1907, and a railway bridge is shown. So it was built between those two dates.'

'1905 in fact,' said Mrs Carstairs. 'No, don't look at me like that, I don't know every date you might want to know. I happened to come across an article on the railway in *Devon Life* last week, and the date stuck, simply because it's the last four digits in my telephone number. But that was a nice bit of historical research. Well done.'

'Look at these,' said Judy. 'Obviously a popular spot to take pictures for postcards, there are two, pretty similar. See there's that boatyard, on the left.' She displayed two black and white pictures of a river scene. In the foreground of each were a couple of boats; there were buildings on the shore in the middle distance, and wooded slopes behind.

Carol came round to look over her shoulder. 'It's Pascoe and Brothers at Wearde Quay – it's still there. You remember Mr Pascoe and his boat from the other day, surely.' Judy did. Carol asked Christine if she has a map showing it.

'Saltash? Yes, 1905 at two thousand five hundred do? Here.' Christine brought the map over to the window.

'That's it, just to the east of the quay there. The slip and that boat house, there. They're working on it right now. Do you remember we saw the yellow JCB on the beach the other day? So when were these taken, or even in what order?'

'Definitely all after 1869,' said Christine. 'You can just make out the western end of the Albert Bridge. And this one was taken before that one.'

'How can you tell that, Sherlock?' demanded Judy.

'The name of the yard. In the earlier one it's just Pascoe, but in the later one it's Pascoe and someone, I can't make it out, but it must be Brothers – Mr Pascoe took on a partner. Elementary, my dear Watson.'

'In that case,' objected Carol, 'how come these trees have shrunk, and what happened to this little house here?'

She tapped Judy's picture with end of her pencil.

Mrs Carstairs came over – she was easily distracted from sticking newspaper cuttings, but who wouldn't be – and offered a magnifying glass. 'This might help,' she said. It did. Under the lens there was far more detail. The earlier picture (if Carol's theory about the trees was right) showed 'Pascoe and Rogers, Boatbuilders', the other, just 'Pascoe'. So when did Mr Pascoe's great-grandfather get rid of his first partner? We assumed that it was a great-grandfather, and that he'd be just as unlikeable as the present Pascoe.

Carol said, 'I think these *Kelly's* will help with this problem. Would you believe that for all the towns in Devon and Cornwall they published an annual list of private residents? All we have to do is look forward and backwards for when Rogers disappeared from the Saltash residents list as a boatbuilder.'

'Yes, but what did you have to be to get included in these lists?' asked Judy, opening one of the massive tomes. 'Only the nobs'll be there, I bet, nothing so common as boatbuilders.'

'Well, I noticed fishmongers in one list, so it can't have been too exclusive.'

Mrs Carstairs interrupted again. 'Don't confuse *Kelly's* with *Who's Who*. It's always been a commercially oriented publication; there's no social cachet or snob value in being in *Kelly's*, any more than being in *Yellow Pages*. May I suggest you look in the classified section under boatbuilders, and start with five-year intervals until you bracket the name change you want, and then you can check year by year?'

'Brilliant, thanks, that'll save time,' said Carol. 'You two going to help?' She looked at Judy and Christine. I was busy with the photographs and lens. 'Good. Judy, here are 1870, 1875. Christine 1880, 1885; I'll do 1890 and '95. Look, I'll show you where it is. In the back here, mmm ... beekeepers, boatbuilders.' She ran her finger down the page. 'OK, we know that in 1895 Pascoe was building boats on his own.'

'And in 1870, he was building them with Mr Rogers. So Carol's right,' said Judy, already thumbing through 1875.

'Yes, and I was wrong,' Christine admitted. 'And Pascoe got rid of Rogers after 1885.'

'Well, it is possible that Mr Rogers died, or just sold out,' objected Mrs Carstairs, who by now had joined them and had pulled 1888 and 1889 off the shelf. 'I am sure Mr Brothers wouldn't like to think the Pascoe family indulges in "getting rid of" partners. Whatever it was, it happened before 1888.'

'And 1887,' said Carol, 'so it must have been 1886, but the 1886 *Kelly's* isn't here.'

'That's a shame,' said Mrs Carstairs. 'I'm afraid we are missing a few volumes.'

I thought we could ask Mr Pascoe, thinking he might know something of his family history, and we had to start somewhere in talking to the locals – although he was not the ideal person to begin with. So we photocopied the postcards, and a few other views, and as our stomachs and watches coincided in saying it was lunchtime, we thanked Mrs Carstairs and left to meet Aunt Liz in town.

We met as arranged at a newly-opened vegetarian restaurant – chosen not only to accommodate Judy's latest fad, but also so Aunt Liz could write something on it for the *Sentinel*. She had just finished looking round the kitchen with the owner when we arrived, and was impressed. She reckoned we should have a decent lunch – which we did, much interrupted by our rather incoherent account of the morning's work. Although we had not learnt much specifically, we had laid some good sound foundations in getting to know our way round the sources we were going to have to use, and somewhat to our surprise we had enjoyed ourselves doing it.

Judy produced the reproductions of the postcards. 'What a super-looking boat,' was Aunt Liz's reaction to the earlier photograph. We had been so busy trying to date it we hadn't noticed the schooner being built in Pascoe and Roger's yard. As she was being constructed parallel to the water, the picture showed her beam view, and very handsome it was – a clipper bow and counter stern, and two enormous raked masts. She was painted a light colour, white or maybe pale grey. 'Perhaps a yacht,' Aunt Liz guessed. 'It really looks quite unlike any of the usual trading schooners they were building in these parts then. Jim'll be interested in that. Will the library let you copy their photos for the project?' she asked.

Judy replied, 'I didn't actually ask. But what I really want to do is to use pictures like this to help painting watercolour views of what it looked like then, which we can put in the project along with a painting of the same view now. That would be better than using photographs – I can guarantee the same viewpoint, and with a little artistic licence I think I can accentuate the difference better than a photograph would.'

'Are you that good?' Aunt Liz wanted to know. We assured her she was. 'In that case you must see the City art gallery – they've got some good Victorian Plymouth scenes there, so you can crib some of their pictures too.'

That came as something of a surprise to Judy, who had regarded Plymouth as something of an artistic backwater. She has gone to the lengths of consulting the lists of exhibitors at the Royal Academy, and had been disappointed at the lack of Plymouthians. That was put right after lunch when Aunt Liz detoured on the way home to give us a quick tour of the gallery. Judy was quite excited, and became very enthusiastic about her 'Then and Now' pictures. Carol, on the other hand, who is a bit of a Philistine and was prepared to be simply bored, took one look at an enormous picture entitled *Fish Sale on a Cornish Beach* and was captivated by the fish. 'Look at the size of them,' she said. 'Don't catch many like that these days. And these too.' She had moved on to a picture of Plymouth fish market. 'We'll have to look at nineteenth-century fishing boats, and methods, won't we? That should be fun.' We were getting gripped by the project, which earlier had appeared as a blight on the holiday.

Back at Saltash, we found Uncle Jim and David Williams deeply engrossed in the brochure for Pascoe and Brothers. So Aunt Liz offered to take us out creek-crawling in *Evenstar*. The wind had eased, and the rain stopped, promising a fine evening.

Aunt Liz is a particularly good sailor, in some ways better than Uncle Jim. She has a real feel for a boat, is very gentle on the helm because she always gets the balance right, and can even get a Drascombe Lugger to move in light airs. She had Olympic ambitions in her teens, but wasn't quite heavy and strong enough to take on the men in Finns – the single-handed dinghy they raced then. But you should see her sailing up muddy creeks – most people run aground before they realise the centreplate is in the putty, but Aunt Liz can feel it long before the boat stops, and she is terrific at tweaking the last bit of lift out of each tack when beating up a narrow channel.

We could even justify creek-crawling as project work. Before the railways, boats were the main means of transport in the Tamar estuary system, and every inlet seems to have a quay – we should certainly have to look at them. As it was getting late we did not go far that afternoon, just up to Wivelscombe lake. The wind was flooky in the lee of the hill with Ince Castle on the top, but the flood helped us beat into what wind there was towards an impossibly narrow gap where the old railway line had crossed the creek – the bridge fortunately now dismantled. With the aid of a three-metre bamboo pole to check the depth – instinct is all very well, but science should not be ignored – and a few judicious strokes on the oars, we reached the quay.

'God knows how they used to work the old stone boats up to places like this,' Aunt Liz commented. 'I suppose the creek has silted up in a hundred years, but even so, you have to admit they must have been pretty good. And you ought to see the size of boat they took up to Morwellham, miles up the river. You'll have to visit that – perhaps Jim knows someone there. And talking of the old man, it's about time we got back. David's staying for supper, and I think Jim's asked Michael Carter too.'

Much though the purist in us rebelled, we motored out; the light airs were not enough to push against the flood.

Uncle Jim and David had stopped working by the time we returned, and were sitting on the garden wall with Michael, each clutching a can of beer. So we had to put up with a certain amount of ribbing as we picked up the mooring under power. 'Any more of your help, Jim Thomson, and you can cook the supper yourself,' Aunt Liz laughed, as she stepped ashore.

'You're on,' he replied. 'I suppose you'd count reminding you that the ensign's still flying as help. Anyway, it's done. David and I cracked the brochure an hour ago, everything's ready to go. If you ladies care to prepare for dinner, it will be ready when you are.'

This was rather a surprise as it was a well-known fact that Uncle Jim was capable of burning a boiled egg. Michael, however, had just completed part of his training which had required him to spend some time in the ship's galley, and reckoned he knew it all. In fact the end results were surprisingly good.

'Easy,' he said. 'I just followed the recipe. Liz had written on the memo pad, "Stuffed Peppers", so that's what I did.'

'The Navy's teaching you something useful then. And being able to read and obey instructions must be useful, even for a naval officer,' Aunt Liz chided him.

Michael grunted. He was having problems with his rule of the road. It seemed he had to pass an exam in it, which makes sense when you think of it, and his navigator was threatening him with stoppage of leave if he didn't improve in the next progress test in two weeks' time.

'Come on, Mike,' Uncle Jim tried to encourage him. 'It's a piece of cake. The girls can hack it – though not to the degree of detail you need, I admit. Why don't you take David under your wing? He needs to know his rule of the road, and he's a very quick learner. In fact I wouldn't be surprised if he couldn't get a better score than you in a fortnight. It's always easier to learn in pairs anyway.'

Michael and David agreed. They were getting along very well, and had already decided that Michael would take over boat-handling instruction. Michael cheered up considerably; now that Uncle Jim had taken charge of the problem, it was bound to go away.

Then we were quizzed on our day's work. We pulled out the picture of Pascoe and Rogers' boatyard, and Uncle Jim was indeed interested in the schooner being built.

'A pity you can't make out the name,' Michael said. He explained that a friend of his, also in the Navy, had broken his arm and had to work ashore. As he too was still under training, he couldn't be gainfully employed in a real job, but the computer skills he acquired at university were being used in the National Maritime Museum in London. They were participating in an international project to index every ship known, linking a number of computers in museums and research establishments round the world, and of course Lloyd's.

'The programming and networking are apparently difficult and complex, and he's a wheel on that sort of thing. The project's far from complete, but if you give him a name, and approximate date of building or loss, he might be able to find it.'

'*Ariel*,' announced Christine. 'Same as Jean-Pierre's Hillyard. I noticed it when we were looking at the picture through the magnifying glass and thought, that's a coincidence.'

Michael scribbled the name and 1886 on a paper napkin and stuffed it in his pocket. But in fact I found out what happened to *Ariel* first – or at least part of the story.

4

As predicted, Mr Pascoe proved most unhelpful. 'Never heard of it. Waste of your time looking. Now stop wasting my time.' We didn't push it – *Ariel* was probably a blind alley – and got on with other work. For the next two weeks we actually worked quite hard, although some of it was rather fun. Uncle Jim did know someone at Morwellham and persuaded him to let us sail up there instead of going by car. We became very chummy with Mrs Carstairs in the library, and she helped us chase all sorts of good (and bad) leads.

For instance, we found a tidal millpond in Millbrook when we were creek-crawling around St John's Lake. It looked just like the one on Forder Creek, but when we sailed in we found no trace of the mill buildings, even after we landed and poked around in the bushes. Next day Christine pulled out the maps of the area – we were trusted on our own in the map cupboards by then – even finding a ten thou sheet of 1890, but they all showed our pond as dry land, with traces of a stream on it. Mrs Carstairs was evidently working on our behalf when we weren't in the library because she announced the solution the next day. She had found in a little local history book that a German bomb had landed on the causeway in 1941 and the sea had reclaimed the meadow – must have been quite a surprise for the farmer the next morning.

We even had the opportunity to show our local knowledge off. One of the local rowing clubs has an enormous clinker-built skiff called the *Anne Glanville*. We were admiring her on the waterfront in Saltash one morning when a muscular young man said, in an irritatingly patronising way, we were probably wondering who Anne Glanville was.

'Oh no,' Judy said airily. 'We know all about her being the best oarsman on the river and her and her all-woman crew rowing across the Channel to beat the French Navy, and then rowing back to a royal reception in 1849.' Nose disjointed, Mr Muscles retired. Uncle Jim deflated our egos, though, when we told him the story, by digging out a magazine article which said it was mostly legend, and the reality was less sensational.

But to return to the *Ariel*. I was looking at gravestones in St Stephen's Church in Saltash when I found a monument, no grave, to Daniel Rogers, loving husband to Mary, and father to his sons William and Albert, who died with him at sea in the *Ariel*, 17 August 1886. With that date it was easy to find a report in the *Western Morning News* of the loss. She was built to be a fruit carrier – which accounts for her unusually fast lines and light-coloured livery – and would have been one of the first banana boats had she not been lost on her maiden voyage with all hands, who included Daniel Rogers, partner of Pascoe, and his two sons. Her loss was a mystery because she was well found, and the weather for the period she must have been lost was good. A lifebelt was found near the Lizard on the eighteenth, two days after she had sailed, which accounted for the date on the memorial.

Jean-Pierre reappeared on one of his occasional

stays about the same time, and asked us all to come sailing with him. Uncle Jim, who can at times be quite old-fashioned, suggested that he should go too, to which Jean-Pierre readily agreed. The Hillyard had a four-berth after cabin which we would be crammed into, complete with minute heads containing the trusty old baby Blake marine loo. The men lorded it in the main saloon.

As we were then in summer proper, with no real wind to speak of, but a reliable sea breeze coming up mid-morning, we only went as far as Newton Ferrers. We left the Tamar just after high water on the Saturday morning, carrying the tide out through the breakwater.

Jean-Pierre had a chart of the English Channel, Western Portion, out. When he found out that was the only one on board, Uncle Jim was a little surprised. 'Still, better than Atlantic, Eastern Portion,' he muttered. We were utterly confident, Uncle Jim knew these waters intimately, and it never occurred to us that anyone who actually owned something like *Ariel* could be foolhardy – notwithstanding the evidence of Jean-Pierre's grounding on Drake's Island. Cavalier is possibly a better way of describing his attitude to rocks and shoals – he dismissed their danger in such a charming and disarming way. Still, going inside the Mewstone at low water was not really a prudent idea, even if it did cut a great corner off the journey. It was fortunate there was so little wind, and the water was clear enough to be able to see the rocks before we hit them. Uncle Jim was less than impressed and, I could see, quite relieved to get through safely. At least at low water there is no temptation to wander outside the main channel when entering the Yealm, and we picked up a visitor's mooring at Newton

Ferrers without incident. This was real cruising, even if not very far, and we certainly didn't let a bit of irresponsibility on the part of the skipper mar our enjoyment of the weekend.

After a gentle drift back on Sunday – going outside the Mewstone, where we caught some mackerel – Jean-Pierre dropped us back at Pascoe and Brothers. We had left *Evenstar* on the mooring he was using, and from there it was just a short motor back to the Thomson house. There we found David's *Red Dragon* on the mooring, and David and Michael in the kitchen with Aunt Liz cleaning fish. They had spent the day at sea, returning with half a dozen fine bass.

'Leave not stopped then, Mike?' Uncle Jim asked him.

'No, navigator was very impressed – ninety-eight per cent in Friday's progress test. I have you and David to thank, though. A bit of competition seems to have done the trick, and we actually learned quite a lot by setting up a training program on one of David's computers. He's got it to produce a random series of combinations of lights and you have to type in what it is – sailing vessel under way, under twenty metres, that sort of thing. It's brilliant.'

'And possibly worth developing and selling,' suggested Uncle Jim.

'I've thought of that,' David replied. 'Nautical Publishing is interested.'

Michael interrupted. 'Before I forget, I've got something for you girls about that schooner that was supposed to have sunk in 1886. Here.'

He passed a neatly typed sheet of paper from his friend in London. He had found an extraordinary story. While on a surveying expedition in the Pacific in 1898, HMS *Magpie* had received intelligence that a slaver was operating around the islands. They had come across a 150-foot two-masted schooner, clipper bows and counter stern, and after a chase they were lucky to win, they boarded her to find she was indeed engaged in the slave trade, although empty at the time. The master was Portuguese and the crew a mixture of harbour scum from all over the world. The ship had no name on the counter and no registration documents, but a sharp-eyed member of *Magpie*'s crew had found *'Ariel'* carved in a beam in the Captain's cabin, and being a West Countryman had recognised the workmanship as Cornish. The log of the *Magpie* had more details of her dimensions and it certainly looked like our *Ariel*. Nothing more had come of the incident, however, as with the connivance of one of the island administrators all the crew of the slaver were unceremoniously hanged and the ship burnt. Although done with the best of motives (at least from the Victorian point of view), this was beyond their authority, and the whole affair was hushed up.

This was quite exciting. *Ariel* must have been taken by pirates on her maiden voyage, we surmised. Or perhaps Rogers had not died and had taken to a life of crime on the high seas. Judy's picture of *Ariel* being built was immediately renamed *The Last British Slaver?*

For supper there was bass for six and mackerel for two, which caused considerable debate over how to decide who was to have what, eventually concluded by recourse to a 'horse'. This is a rather childish game played by naval officers, in which you have to guess a number selected by one person. Each person takes it in turn to guess, with the holder of the horse saying whether the number is high or low.

If you get the number, you lose. Well, I thought it childish, but perhaps I'm biased – I lost; but so did Mike, whose idea it was, which made me feel better.

When we'd finished, David wanted to see how we were getting on with the project. We fired up Uncle Jim's PC and showed him. We had become quite adept at working it by then, having made all the usual mistakes at first, and learnt the hard way to save often, and always make a back-up. That made David laugh. 'Everyone learns that the hard way,' he said. 'I like the map. Yours, Christine?'

Christine was very proud of her map. She'd spent ages drawing it on the graphics application, but the effort had been worthwhile, because once she'd got it we could take chunks of it, and import them into the text, and highlight different bits to show the spread of towns, or the railways or whatever.

'Have you tried this?' he asked. 'With this you can really work in fine detail, pixel by pixel. See.' He clicked away with the mouse for a couple of minutes and smoothed out some of Christine's curves, and deleted the spiky bits where she'd overrun and couldn't get the eraser in to tidy up.

'Fantastic,' she said. 'Thanks. Give me a go.'

So of course we all had to have a go as well, but in spite of that, Christine succeeded in real improvements in her map.

'Just goes to show what you can do if you read the manual,' David said. 'But you could do a lot more with a better printer – all these colours you see will just come out black on this machine. Now, if I were putting this on the Desktop Publisher, I'd lay it out like this.' He doodled on a scrap of paper. 'Then all these interesting bits which you can't fit in the narrative, instead of being footnotes, which are boring, can be put in separate boxes, like this, and with a different background colour or shading. And then you can extract them in big letters in the middle of the column.'

He pulled out the Sunday paper colour supplement to show us what he meant.

'And Judy's pictures, we could scan. That means we would have a digital map of it, and then you can put it where you like, and change the shape and size to fit the test. Or you could tone it down and use it for background for the text.'

'Do you think there's any chance?' I asked tentatively.

David looked embarrassed, but Uncle Jim saved him.

'Sally, girls,' he said, 'have you any idea what it would cost? You can't expect David's firm, which is still finding its feet, to stand that sort of expense. Isn't that right, David?'

'I'm afraid so,' he said, clearly unhappy at having to say no. 'We do have a sort of unwritten rule that any of us can do private work, or for friends, but we have to pay for it at cost. And Jim's right, this would be pricy.'

'Go on then, how much?' asked Judy.

'I bet none of you would be anywhere near,' Mike interrupted. 'Come on, write your guesses down while David works out the answer. I'll buy you a pint if you're within ten per cent.'

'We don't drink pints,' said Judy archly. 'We're ladies.'

But she grabbed a piece of paper and pencil and started scribbling.

David started skimming through the documents

on the computer. 'How close to finishing are you?' he asked.

I told him we'd probably done about three-quarters of the research, but only turned about a tenth of the way into anything like the final product.

'And there are eight of Judy's before-and-after paintings, I think you said?' Judy nodded. 'The maps aren't a problem. About twenty pages, a copy of each, and one for the school, nice cover, binding. I don't think there would be much change from £200.'

We all gasped. Mike chuckled. Our nearest guess had been £50 – Christine's. 'Just what you'd expect from women,' he said. 'No idea of the price of anything. Pity your husbands.'

It was said in fun, admittedly, with the intention of getting a reaction, which it was about to get. Judy was really quite wound up and about to leap into the attack, but Aunt Liz smoothed things over.

'For that sort of money, you'd need a sponsor,' she murmured vaguely. 'Any ideas? I can think of someone who might leap at the opportunity to forge a partnership between industry and education, the public and private sectors, to nurture our greatest investment for the future – the minds of the young,' she continued in an exaggeratedly pompous manner.

'Got it?' Uncle Jim and David exclaimed together. 'I think you might be right. Clever girl,' Uncle Jim went on. 'Come on, you lot, don't you recognise who she means? Bit pompous, means well, minor political and true blue ambitions?'

'Not Mr Brothers?' Carol asked.

'The very same,' Aunt Liz replied. 'It really is just up his street, and although I might have sounded as if I was taking the mickey, I do in fact have a lot of time for him – he may not be a real local, but he's doing more for this area than many who are.'

Judy wanted to know if Mr Brothers' partner Pascoe was likely to prove difficult, and Uncle Jim admitted he could be. However, David found the solution to that problem.

'Properly presented, you might get local television interested,' he suggested. 'I mean, there's not a lot of real news at the moment, is there?'

'No, even Jason's slave traders seem to have gone on holiday,' Aunt Liz admitted. 'Jim, don't you know someone on the local commercial channel?'

He did, of course, and as an ad on the television during the early evening would cost about £2, 000 a minute, he guessed, even the notoriously stingy and unhelpful Pascoe should see the economic sense of a free slot.

It was decided that tomorrow we would write a letter to Mr Brothers, and Uncle Jim would chat up his friend at the local TV station. If he got a favourable response he would deliver our letter in the afternoon when he had to go to the boatyard to discuss the job he was doing for them. We would have the opportunity to push our case in the evening if he reckoned we were in with a chance; we were due in the library the next day.

Then we were packed off to bed.

None of us had written a begging letter before – Uncle Jim thought it good training for us – and we struggled with it for about an hour after breakfast. Eventually Uncle Jim pronounced himself satisfied with it – it was polite, stated what we wanted and why, and why we thought Pascoe and Brothers should contribute. 'They need to know what's in it for them,' he explained as he dropped us at the station to get the local train into Plymouth. 'Don't worry. It's a good letter, well presented, but if you don't get the money, you're no worse off than before, and there may be other sources to tap.'

Hardly surprisingly, we did not work particularly well that day. Even Mrs Carstairs shared our excitement, agreeing that it would be tremendous fun to see the project really well presented. She would be very happy to see a copy of it on her shelves if there was any chance of producing an extra one. We were a bit dubious – £40 a copy seemed a bit steep to try and get more. We said we'd ask though, particularly after she exclaimed that the more copies produced the cheaper each one is; it's all something to do with fixed and variable costs, which explains why something like *Yachting Monthly* doesn't cost about £100 each, a thing which had been puzzling us a little.

We returned to Saltash and good news. Uncle Jim's chum had recently moved into the news production team and was well placed to influence what was worth covering – he also thought it would make a nice story anyway. So when Uncle Jim had tried the idea on Mr Brothers he had quite a powerful back-up argument. He hadn't needed it though. Mr Brothers had liked the partnership of industry and education line, and fostering an awareness of our heritage and its importance to contemporary events – we had laid it on rather thick, I must admit. Mr Pascoe had been less easy to persuade to listen to us, but the possibility of £2,000 worth of advertising for a tenth of that made him relent somewhat. It seemed Jean-Pierre had pleaded our cause too.

But Uncle Jim was not going to give us anything on a plate. All he had done was prepare the ground, he said – he had given us the opportunity to be heard; we had to do the actual persuading. That meant we had two hours before Pascoe and Brothers would be coming round for drinks with the Thomsons, and a presentation from us on what we were doing, and what we'd like to be able to do. After the initial panic it was not as difficult as all that. We did at least know the work we had already done pretty thoroughly, and we had talked about little else during the day, but now we could make it look really good. We'd been through all the magazines in the library, raiding them for good ideas, and hoped that David's machines were sophisticated enough.

Fortunately he was coming round too, and was able to confirm that everything we wanted was possible – if not necessarily desirable. We were after some fairly violent mixtures of typefaces – fonts, he called them – and layouts, sometimes on the same page, which he recommended toning down.

'Don't underestimate the value of blank space on a page,' he said. 'It breaks things up into easily digestible chunks – don't imagine that people are likely to want to read the whole thing in one go – and it's jolly useful for emphasising something. Now, have you got a title, and any ideas for a cover design?'

A good question, and one which I had given no thought to at all, but Judy and Christine had.

'We haven't talked to Sally and Carol,' Christine began, 'but as they're not the artistic types, we weren't sure how much they could contribute.'

Carol and I snorted, but could not fail to recognise the truth of what she said.

Christine continued, 'If it's possible, we'd like the outline map of the Tamar, very faint, with a detail from one of Judy's paintings superimposed on it. This bit here.' She used some pieces of paper to blank out parts of Judy's impression of Kingsand full of ships waiting for the tide. The detail was of the bows of a schooner, its anchor cable taut in the current.

'Mm. It can be done, but it may be too fussy. Worth trying. I'd have to...' David had picked up the bits of paper and was muttering to himself. 'Sorry,' he said, 'it's an interesting problem. What about a title?'

'We've thought of that too.' Judy and Christine had obviously been getting their heads together. 'How about that bit from *Julius Caesar* we did in English last term?

'There is a tide in the affairs of men,
Which, taken at the flood, leads on to fortune.'

Uncle Jim finished the quotation:

'Omitted, all the voyage of their life
Is bound in shallows and in miseries.
On such a full sea are we now afloat;
And we must take the current when it serve
Or lose our ventures.'

'Brilliant idea, Judy. It's entirely appropriate to the Victorian attitude, although I'm not sure how much they'd appreciate being compared to Brutus,' he added.

'Surely not the whole quotation,' I objected. 'It would hardly be a handy title.'

'No, silly, just the first bit, which everyone knows. Not everyone can rattle off the rest of it like your uncle.'

'Wouldn't we be better using a bit that's not so familiar – make people think a bit?' Carol wondered.

'Yes, you would,' David answered, with Uncle Jim nodding agreement. 'And then you put the full quotation inside, so people can recognise the bit they've half remembered, convince themselves they knew it all along, and that they're jolly clever and cultured. Then they're on your side straight away. It's amazing what you get from a carefully massaged ego.'

'What about *In Shallows and in Misery*?' Carol laughed. 'If Judy had had her way about how horrible and unjust the Victorians were, that would have been entirely appropriate.'

That was about to start an argument, but Christine chipped in with *'Taken at the Flood,'* which was also appropriate to our imaginary voyage up the river. So it was agreed.

The briefing to Pascoe and Brothers was a lot less of a trial than we had feared. For a start, it was hardly formal enough to be called a briefing, just a social chat really, as it quickly became clear that they had already made up their minds. I suspect Uncle Jim had done a better job for us than he was admitting. Mr Brothers appeared interested in a mildly condescending way – although Aunt Liz said that was just because, as a bachelor, he was not entirely as ease with kids, even grown-up ones like us. He also suggested we might call round to the yard one day to look at the books as they still had all the accounts for the firm back to something like 1830, and it was his idea that we should do it when his partner was out. He's not that lacking in sensitivity.

Mr Pascoe asked one or two questions, didn't listen to the answers and then buttonholed Uncle Jim in the corner. Jean-Pierre was flatteringly interested in the whole thing, and was most amused that we might have located the last slaver built in Britain, and had caught out Queen Victoria's Navy in hanging its last users without trial. 'This captain should have been a Frenchman, he has the love of liberty and a true Gallic disregard for petty authority – but it would have been more difficult in a French ship, the guillotine is not so easy to use on a rolling deck.'

Mind you, they were all very interested next day, when Uncle Jim's friend in the TV station was as good as his word and sent the local news team round. Not that they all wanted to be on television themselves, but rather all the men wanted a chance to chat up Sue Sawyer, the presenter.

We were filmed sailing up and down the river a bit, and then gave some details to a keen and spotty young man with a notebook, who took himself terribly seriously. One might have expected an excess of interest in Sue from Mr Pascoe, who, in spite of his rudeness, has something of a reputation with women. Mr Brothers, as he was paying, was entitled to push the boatyard, and his views on industry, education etc, so that he'd be noticed by the election selectors, and could be excused for trying to monopolise her. Michael Carter had found some excuse to get away from his ship – he claimed that as ship's Public Relations Officer he was just increasing his contacts. I think it was closeness of contact he was after. At least he is young and single, though, unlike Uncle Jim, who was just as bad as the rest of them; which made me really cross.

I found Aunt Liz in the kitchen, her shoulders shaking, and tried to comfort her.

'Come on,' I said, 'don't let it get you down. But how can he do that? They're all like flies round rotten meat.'

But Aunt Liz had not been upset, she had retired to the kitchen unable to contain a fit of giggles. 'You're so right,' she spluttered, 'but I think bees round a honey pot is more charitable. You have to admit she's an attractive girl, and she's a journalist: it's her job to get people to want to talk to her. Anyway, Jim will be so overcome with remorse at behaving like a young lieutenant at a cocktail party that I shouldn't wonder if I got flowers tonight, or even, champagne if he's feeling really guilty.'

Then she shoved me back out of the kitchen, with a tray of sandwiches. The camera crew fell on them like seagulls following a trawler, then left to get some shots of Pascoe and Brothers' yard before going to cover a traffic jam, or something equally exciting. The two partners left with them, and Jean-Pierre, who was off again back to France. David had arrived, but seemed impervious to Sue's long blonde hair, and big blue eyes, as he was engrossed in conversation with keen and spotty.

Someone had just told Sue about the *Ariel*, so I joined in the quite lively and deep discussion that was going on about slavery. I had to admit that Aunt Liz was right – Sue was good at getting people to talk to her. She didn't talk down to us, and took our views seriously, but would cut in with a challenge if we were on shaky ground – she'd have made a brilliant teacher, and we were genuinely sorry to see her go.

After the time and effort the TV company put in that morning with us, it was hardly surprising that we had good coverage on the local magazine programme after the six o'clock news. David and Michael had come round again to watch it.

'Not bad,' Uncle Jim commented.

'Not bad?' Michael echoed. 'She's gorgeous.'
'Typical, one-track mind. No, the story, I mean.'
'Really?' Aunt Liz raised an eyebrow.
'Of course,' Uncle Jim went on, 'what I meant was that everyone got everything they wanted.' Aunt Liz winked at me and shifted her glance to the roses in a vase by the window. 'Pascoe and Brothers have a jolly good plug for their craftsman-finished boats, the Lynher 35s, and Mr Brothers' political orthodoxy will have impressed someone.'
'Even David got a mention,' said Judy, with a hint of bitterness. 'But what about us? It's our project, and all we heard about that was the business about *Ariel*. I mean, it's interesting, but hardly important. Effective town planning practically eradicating cholera in a generation is much more significant.' Judy had quite changed camps over the Victorians in the last few weeks, and was about to get going. This time it was Michael who saved us.
'I didn't. Didn't even get her telephone number.' He sighed and then laughed.
'654321,' said David.
Michael gaped at him.
'It's in the phone book. You look up the TV company, and there it is, and when you get through to the switchboard, you ask for Sue,' David explained.
'Where no doubt you come up against a protective cohort of agents and secretaries keeping young Romeos like Mike away,' continued Uncle Jim.
'No doubt,' said David with a smile.
'Now, what do you think a girl like that does after she's read the news?' Michael was not to be put off.
'Goes home to a husband and kids, and a sinkful of washing-up, I bet.' Judy was not being charitable.
'No, she's not married, I found that much out.'

'Actually,' interrupted David, 'she's going to the Theatre Royal tonight, to the opera. And so am I, so I'd better be off.'

Michael spluttered. 'Opera? You never said you liked opera. Verdi, isn't it, this week?'

'That's right, *Rigoletto*. It's the Welsh National Opera, and my brother's singing Marulio. So when I heard that Sue had failed to get a ticket, I said I thought I might be able to help, and I could. We're in the fifth row of the stalls.'

'But you hardly spoke to her,' I objected. 'I thought you were the only one not chasing her, you spent ages talking to the reporter.'

'That's right. I had to make sure he got South West Graphics' details right – it was he who told me Sue hadn't got tickets. So I didn't need to talk to her for long. Must go. Bye.' And he left.

The stunned silence had just been broken by everyone laughing at once when the phone rang. Uncle Jim took it.

'Whoops,' he said when he got back. 'I've just had a mild roasting from your Miss Welford – we didn't think about checking with her first, did we?' We hadn't.

'Should have realised that Dorset is in the same TV region, and that she might see it. Fortunately she liked it, and thinks it's a great idea, and thought the girls came over very well as representatives of the school. But I wouldn't like to be on the wrong side of her when she's not pleased.' We agreed.

'Oh, and she said she wouldn't be fooled by well-presented rubbish.'

Judy started to splutter, but Uncle Jim stopped her. 'I think she was only joking, and anyway, what you've done so far is not rubbish. And another thing.

I'll let you into a secret. Everyone's fooled by well-presented rubbish. I should know, I do it for a living.'

The phone rang again, and Aunt Liz took it. This time it was Mr Brothers, to say how much he'd enjoyed our slot on the television, and as his partner was travelling to the Midlands next day – there was an unexpected delay in production of hulls for the Lynher 35s – would we like to come and look at the firm's records tomorrow? Indeed we would. Aunt Liz thanked him for us, and fixed for us to call about ten o'clock.

5

Getting to Pascoe and Brothers' yard is either an hour's walk round the head of the creek, or a twenty-minute drive, or we could take *Evenstar*. As Aunt Liz had to be at Looe fish market at some unearthly hour – a trip Carol was loath to give up – the car was not available. None of us really fancied the walk, so we were delighted that Uncle Jim was persuaded to let us take the boat. The tide was not really right – high water was about midday – and there was hardly a breath of wind, so we had to motor round. At least that meant we could guarantee being on time, in spite of a slight delay resulting from catching a single mackerel, and Carol insisting that where there's one there must be others which we ought to try for. We towed the dinghy to row ashore in, leaving *Evenstar* on one of the yard's buoys, fairly close to Mr Pascoe's half-decked keelboat.

The yard itself was the usual clutter of planks, bits of ironmongery, and one or two boats still ashore in spite of the sailing season being well advanced. But the new shed where the Lynher 35s were being finished was extremely clean and tidy and modern-looking, with none of the traditional boat-building clutter. Mr Brothers took us to his office in the northern end of the shed and introduced us to his secretary.

Wendy had seen us all on the box and was very

impressed and only too keen to help. She cleared a table for us and opened a large metal cabinet.

'There you are – 1830 to 1900. I'm afraid you might find it rather dull, lots and lots of tables of figures, payments and receipts,' she smiled.

'Accounts aren't dull,' objected Mr Brothers. 'The whole life of the company is in here. Sorry,' he apologised to us, 'I'm not primarily a boatbuilder, I'm really an accountant; Mr Pascoe has all the boatbuilding expertise, I just keep the firm on a sound business footing. It seems to work.'

Carol wanted to know how much a boat would have cost then, and with a little searching we found that a 35-foot lugger in 1860 cost between £110 and £120; which we thought was cheap. Christine, however, had been looking at other prices for the project.

'Don't forget that the typical rent for a fisherman's cottage was about £3 a year, and a farm labourer's wages a shilling a day – that's 5p,' she explained. 'So his boat represented a considerable chunk of capital to a fisherman.'

Mr Brothers was most impressed – he'd found a kindred spirit, and soon they were digging through the accounts with enthusiasm.

'Hey, look at this, you two,' she called to Carol and me. 'How long has your uncle Jim's family lived here?'

Not at all we explained, he and Liz had only moved to Saltash after he had left the Navy.

'That's a good thing, because with interest he could owe Mr Pascoe a small fortune – look: "To bad debts, for 29-foot hooker, Walter Thomson of St Stephens, £80, the fourteenth of September 1875",' she read out.

I wanted to know what *Ariel* had cost. We knew

exactly when she was built, so it was no problem finding the ledgers covering August 1886. The odd thing was that no one appeared to have paid for her. We found a few entries for items bought for her, including one which surprised us. £20 had been paid for *quincaillerie* to a Monsieur Le Braz of Brest.

'They're something to eat, aren't they?' supposed Carol. 'Little birds – quails, I think.'

'What do you do in French classes – think about your stomach all the time?' Christine objected. 'You're thinking of *caille* – that's French for quail. *Quincaillerie* is French for ironmongery. They must have bought nails and stuff from Monsieur Le Braz.

'Odd that, you'd have thought they could have got those quite easily nearer home – and cheaper.' Mr Brothers had taken an interest. 'See these entries for nails? They seem to have bought them fairly regularly, every other month.'

Carol might not have known much French, but she did know a bit about old boats, and she had specialised in this area in the project. She reckoned that with *Ariel* being such an unusual boat, more like a yacht than the conventional trading schooners they built in these parts, they'd have needed special bits and pieces like cranze and gammon irons, and other obscure bits of metal no one had heard of, and they could perhaps have been found more easily in Brest. She also pointed out that the Cornish and Bretons have always had strong cultural links, so it was hardly surprising. And that seemed a perfectly good enough explanation.

Mr Brothers let us photocopy a few pages from the ledgers; we made some more notes, said thank you and left for home.

The sea breezes had filled in, and as the tide had

hardly turned we sailed back, an easy reach that probably got us back not appreciably later than if we had motored – and we caught the other mackerel which Carol insisted had been there all the time. The rest of the day was spent working. With a midday high water we could only have gone out towards the Sound. No creek-crawling on the ebb, and we'd still have had a bit of tide against us on the way back unless we were going to be late. So we were feeling quite self-righteous after stopping about six, lounging in the garden with Uncle Jim and Aunt Liz.

The phone rang. Uncle Jim took it. He reappeared after about five minutes, settled back in his chair and picked up his can of beer. He was building up the suspense deliberately – you could see that from his face.

Aunt Liz cracked. 'Well?'

'A very odd call,' he said. It had been Mr Brothers on the phone. He wanted Uncle Jim to take Pascoe's keelboat in the regatta tomorrow. The yard had been represented every year since nineteen thirty-something, and his partner couldn't do it this year because he'd just leapt off to France. Apparently when Mr Pascoe returned that evening, there had been quite a row about us being allowed to look at the books, especially anything affecting *Ariel*; and when Mr Brothers had said there was no chance of them backing out of the sponsoring deal, Mr Pascoe said he was getting the night ferry to Roscoff. Mr Brothers knew nothing about sailing the boat, and even if Uncle Jim didn't win, at least tradition would have been upheld.

'What did you say?' we all demanded of Uncle Jim. Of course he'd agreed; I knew he would, it was obvious he'd always wanted to sail that boat. But who was to crew?

'Liz, you'll helm?' he said.

'Love to. What's the opposition like?'

'No idea. At the very most there will be five of the one-designs racing, and we get our own start, so it should be quite fun.'

'Just like the old days. How many crew do these things take?'

Now that was the question I wanted answering.

'Three. The third had better be Sally.' He turned to me. 'You've got more racing experience than the others – fancy it?'

Did I ever!

'But don't forget these won't handle like anything you're used to. You can't flick them round like the Lasers you have at school, but, unlike the Lugger, it will accelerate if you get a puff. Oh and it has a spinnaker,' he added as an afterthought. 'We'll have to practise early tomorrow.'

The others were disappointed, particularly Carol, who is keen on old boats, but as even she admitted, they were all cruising types; and as I was the only one foolish enough to carry on racing right through the winter term, I ought to be the one to go.

Our start was at 10.15, but as Uncle Jim had said, we needed to see what all the ropes and things did, so we were up and about much earlier. Carol had eventually persuaded him that she should be allowed to take *Evenstar* while we were racing, and she gave us three a lift to Pascoe and Brothers' moorings to collect the boat – *Maud*, she was called. Apparently they all had girls' names, quite fashionable ones in their day, I suppose. There was *Maud, Hermione, Flora, Victoria* and *Mary*.

Mr Brothers was there to see us off and wish us luck – but not to sail. He was definitely a social sailor, so his part in the regatta was to be polite and charming to all the right people in the yacht club. Something he's probably very good at, Uncle Jim reckoned, but without malice. After all, someone had to do it (I still don't really see why – perhaps that's something you only get let into when you're grown up) and rather Mr Brothers than him.

We had a good two hours to get used to the boat. The wind was south westerly force three, although forecast to back and drop later. So we had perfect conditions for getting the kite – racespeak for spinnaker – up and down, lots of times, which was just as well as the first time we did it, it took every bit of rope in the boat up with it – a frightful mess. And we went round buoys, with and without the kite, and putting it up and taking it down at the same time as going round, until Uncle Jim decided he and I, who were doing all the work, had had enough. Not that Aunt Liz was being idle. Once she'd got the measure of how much way the boat needed for a tack, it was a question of judging any manoeuvre against how fast we could manage sail changes.

'See what happens if we're slow on the gybe, and the helmsman doesn't notice, and gets the main over early,' Uncle Jim said after one of our early attempts, when the spinnaker had wrapped itself round the forestay.

We were getting quite slick by the time we started thinking about the start, but of course in the race it would all be fouled up by other boats trying to do the same things in the same place.

The start was above the bridges, with the signals

being given from a committee boat. Uncle Jim grumbled that the timing could have been improved upon. With a bit of thought, the yacht club could have picked a weekend when the start didn't have to be when the tide was at its strongest. But he shut up when Aunt Liz pointed out that his superior tidal knowledge should help redress the balance of less experience of this boat.

We watched the start before ours to see which end of the line was better. It has been well laid, with little bias, and as Uncle Jim predicted, most boats elected to start on starboard, at the eastern, slightly uptide end, by the committee boat, and we reckoned to do the same. In the five minutes between starts we did a couple of dummy runs. I looked after the jib, and the stop-watch; Uncle Jim had the main and fed Aunt Liz with the position, course and speed of any boats likely to affect us and what she should do about it; this left her free to concentrate on boat speed. It seemed to work well – but only, I guessed, because they were used to it. I made a mental note to ask them where and when they had raced together.

Uncle Jim had been watching the other boats in our class practising their starts. 'They're line shy,' he said. 'What do you think?'

I had not heard the expression before, and said so.

'He means that they're frightened of being over the line on the start, so they hang back,' Aunt Liz explained. 'And he's thinking that we could start by roaring round the back of the committee boat on port, stick in a last minute tack between the inner distance mark and the rest of the fleet, and start in pole position, on starboard, lee-bowing them all. Right?'

'Spot on,' he said. 'OK?'

Relying on the other boats not getting their starts right struck me as being a bit risky, but I wasn't prepared to say so, unlike Aunt Liz.

'No,' she said firmly. (Actually she was less ladylike than that.) 'Fair enough in your own boat, and I know we got away with it a couple of times in the Flying Fifteen, but not in someone else's, and especially not one as fragile as this.'

'Have it your own way. Harumph.'

I thought Uncle Jim was about to have an uncharacteristic sulk, but he winked at me. 'Worth a try, wasn't it? Time, please.'

'One minute, fifteen seconds,' I told him.

'Let's go round once more and join the procession then,' he said.

For all that, we made a cracking start, not quite in the pole position – there was one boat on our lee bow – but Aunt Liz reckoned she could pinch her way clear of his dirty wind.

'Or I'll have him when he calls for water when we get to the putty,' she said. Concentrated aggression was not something I associated with Aunt Liz.

We all stayed on starboard to get the slacker tide on the Devon side of the river, and hopefully to get less flooky wind than we would get under the lee of Saltash. As we closed the shore I offered to sound – there was a pole marked in feet and inches clipped under the side deck. But Uncle Jim said no, we'd let the other boat do that for us; we would have to go when he called for water, whatever the depth was. Anyway, we were close enough to hear his crew singing out the depths.

Aunt Liz was trying desperately to squeeze every inch to windward. 'Got to have room for a slow tack,' she muttered.

'Water, water!' the helmsman of the other boat shouted, and immediately put his helm down.

Aunt Liz swore, very quietly. 'Tacking,' she said in a more normal voice. But she wasn't to be panicked into a hurried manoeuvre which would cost ground. 'Steady,' she growled at me as I made to smack the jib in to starboard. She had not pushed the helm hard down as the other boat had, but was letting *Maud* come round in a gentle curve. She held her head to wind while she made a good boat's length dead to windward and then brought her all the way round onto the port tack. *Hermione*'s stem passed a handbreadth off our counter. Then we were both off towards Saltash, but with *Hermione* comfortable under our lee.

'Fair enough in your own boat,' Uncle Jim said, grinning at her.

'I'd have had stacks of room if he hadn't tacked before me. Nice though. Got him just where I want him.' She risked a glance away from the sails to look at the other helmsman, and smiled at him. 'That always cracks them,' she said, 'or at least it did when I was younger. Now come on, you two. Jim, that main's oversheeted, and the Cunningham could come down a bit more; and Sally, you can probably get another inch on that jib.'

By the time we passed under the bridges we were five or six boat lengths clear of *Hermione,* who was holding off the rest of the fleet. But nothing that depends on the weather is certain, as Uncle Jim often says. Indeed, he said it then as we sailed into a hole in the wind, and the others didn't. I was practically spitting in frustration, but Uncle Jim and Aunt Liz sat there very calmly.

'You can only sail with the wind you've got. Ease

that jib.' He was easing the main. 'It may have dropped, but it's also lifted. Come down to leeward. Gently,' *Maud* heeled to port, the sails filled, and she was moving again, but in third or fourth place.

'Wind's coming back, and it's a massive heading shift. *Hermione* and *Flora* have both been caught aback.' This was Aunt Liz, who now had the best view as Uncle Jim and I were huddled together by the lee deck. 'I'm going to tack, but it'll have to be quick and gentle.'

She coaxed *Maud* round. I had just let the port sheet go, and the main had crossed the centreline, when the wind came back, only for us it was a lifting shift. Uncle Jim gave me a hand. 'Only just,' he said, 'but good enough.'

Indeed it was. On port, if the wind held, we would weather Henn Point and make it into the Lynher, whereas the others were heading almost straight for the Plymouth shore. Of course the wind didn't hold in that direction, and when it headed us we tacked back onto starboard. The others had also come onto port and then back again, so although we were still astern of them all, we were well to windward. I thought we might have regained the lead, but the others thought *Hermione* still slightly ahead.

Uncle Jim apologised, then stood up to get a better view of the water ahead. He was looking for where the tide split – that was the way he put it – as he wanted to wait until we were in the tide pushing up the Lynher before tacking. *Victoria,* who was definitely last, tacked.

'Too early,' said Uncle Jim. 'He'll be set to the north too much.'

'Always worth taking a risk at the back of the fleet,' Aunt Liz replied. 'Nothing to lose.'

We sailed through a band of scummy, weedy water, which was agreed to be this mysterious tidal split, and tacked. The other three went very shortly afterwards, and sure enough we had made up plenty of ground. All three were astern of us, *Flora* and *Mary* were enjoying a luffing match right astern of us, but *Hermione* was well up to windward, and might still be ahead.

Aunt Liz tweaked her as close to the wind as she could, and I think *Hermione* sacrificed a bit of her weather advantage to get boat speed to try and get ahead of us, so gradually we came together. It was very close – *Hermione*'s bow was level with our mast, about a metre and a half to windward – and we were engaged in a classic luffing duel; sailing the school's Lasers in the reservoir had never been as exciting as this. I was concentrating hard on the jib, Uncle Jim on the main, and Aunt Liz on pinching onto *Hermione*'s lee bow – we had all forgotten *Victoria*.

Suddenly, 'Starboard,' we heard roared from leeward.

'What the–' said Aunt Liz peering under the boom. 'Damn.' She looked quickly over her shoulder. 'No time. Dump the main, Jim. Back the jib,' she shouted as she hauled the tiller up.

Uncle Jim was quicker off the mark than me. He let the main go, then smacked the jib out of the jammer, but by then I'd woken up and grabbed the port sheet. *Maud*, practically stopped, had turned through 90 degrees in less than a boat's length, and *Victoria* shot across our bows. *Hermione*, who could never have responded in time to our call for water if we'd made it, had started to tack, too late to avoid a collision altogether, but fortunately in time for it to be only a glancing blow.

As we got ourselves sorted out, I heard *Victoria*'s helmsman ask *Hermione* if they were retiring.

'Yes,' they replied. 'Any damage?'

'No, just scratched paint. Bad luck.'

'See you in the bar. Owe you one. Go and sort out Pascoe's boat. I don't know where he found totty that can sail, but his latest is pretty good.'

Aunt Liz was in danger of losing concentration. 'Did you hear that? I've not been referred to as totty for years. I think I owe him a beer.'

'Not likely, not to someone that thinks I'm Pascoe,' grumbled Uncle Jim. 'Come on, let's get this old hooker moving again.'

We tacked, and now when we closed *Victoria* we were on starboard, but they were paying more attention than we had been. Even as Uncle Jim filled his lungs, they started to tack: a beautiful, elegant, old-fashioned tack that lost no ground or speed, and put them right on our lee bow. Aunt Liz had been expecting it, and managed a similarly good tack out of their dirty wind.

'He's bloody good,' Aunt Liz murmured. 'If he's got a worked-up crew, he could do well on the marks.'

'Well, we've just got to get there first,' I said.

'Well said. You're learning something at that fancy school. How, do you reckon?' Uncle Jim asked.

The windward mark was on the north shore of the Lynher, about half a kilometre up river of the Thomsons' house. I thought that two more tacks should lay it, and if *Victoria* tacked when we next crossed again, she might overstand the mark, if we judged our next tack right.

'And if we're wrong, she'll have an overlap. But it's worth the risk,' Aunt Liz agreed. 'We've got another half minute or so on this tack.'

Victoria had carried on to the south on starboard, but was tacking as we finished talking. Uncle Jim looked around. 'We'll go as soon as this puff's gone.'

We sailed into the ruffled patch of water and *Maud* accelerated. As the wind dropped again, Aunt Liz gently put the helm down for another smooth tack. We closed *Victoria*, the bearing steady.

'Perhaps a good bellow might panic him into a quick and crummy tack,' Aunt Liz suggested. Uncle Jim tried it, but it didn't work. They executed another faultless tack onto our lee bow, and again we tacked away.

'Very close,' Uncle Jim commented, squinting at the buoy about a hundred metres away, fine on the weather bow. 'The tide should do the rest.'

As I'd hoped, *Victoria* had not thrown a quick tack after ours, but had waited to get it right. After about 20 seconds it looked like we'd got it right.

'The last thing we want now is a heading shift,' Uncle Jim growled at the approaching gust. 'Please, a lift.' He raised his eyes to the heavens. 'Thank you, Lord.' The wind backed slightly, and *Victoria* lost any chance of getting an overlap, and the right to round the mark inside of us. They certainly weren't giving up, though; from where I was sitting, their stem looked like it was glued to our stern.

The next leg was a short reach, straight across the river, which was naturally just a procession with no position changes, before rounding another buoy to port.

Victoria was still hard on our tail after we'd rounded the mark and set the spinnaker for the run up tide back towards the Tamar. *Flora*, I think, was just ahead of *Mary*, but both were still in contention. With three spinnakers set behind us, we were getting some very dirty wind, any one of the others could pick up a puff and get to the front, which was just what happened to *Mary*. But she was then in the same position we had found ourselves in.

As there was still a reasonable breeze going, we had stayed as a bunch out in the river; no one had risked the flooky wind on the southern shore to get out of the tide. However, once past Jupiter Point, the wind started to die, as forecast, and everyone realised the need to look for less contrary currents. We all followed *Mary* into the shallow water to the north and east of Beggar's Island.

'It's very shallow in here, Jim,' Aunt Liz said.

'Yeah, but if we're to take *Mary* we've got to be inside her, and even more out of the tide. He can't risk running aground, so he's got to play it safe. Mind you, the same's true for us. So, young Sally, you get a chance to sound, but keep it quiet, and add six inches onto the depth each time you call it out. We don't want to give anything away, but what we do, we'd rather it was misleading.'

I gave Uncle Jim the spinnaker guy and took out the sounding pole, a three-metre bamboo like *Evenstar*'s but with imperial markings instead of metric.

I asked if he was happy with feet and inches – I didn't think I could manage simultaneous conversions.

'Of course I am. Never really been happy with metres, coloured charts and all that. Passing fad, mark my words.'

'Jim, please, not now.' Aunt Liz got him off one of his favourite hobby horses, and I started swinging the pole ahead of the boat, noting the depth as it passed through the vertical, and calling it out to Uncle Jim.

'Six feet!' I shouted. The water in the Tamar is

rarely clear, and sometimes you can't see the bottom until there's only six inches (or fifteen centimetres to the rest of us).

'Not so loud,' Uncle Jim said, winking at me, and whispering, 'Nice touch.'

I dropped my voice. 'Five eight. Five eight. Five eight. Five seven. Five six.'

'Do you know exactly what this draws?' Aunt Liz asked him.

He didn't, but Mr Brothers had said it was about four foot six. This was borne out by our not being aground in five feet of water, and by *Victoria*, who was obviously listening for my *sotto voce* soundings, edging closer inshore, and gaining slightly, as we were on *Mary*.

'I'm relying on your legendary skill in smelling the bottom,' he replied, grinning at her.

'Thanks a bunch,' she said. 'Well, we're pretty close now. I can feel the helm getting sloppy.'

'Five three,' I called. We were all pretty well stopped now, although the water was still sliding past us.

'Take her in a bit more, Liz.'

'She's on,' she said.

I made to dive across to leeward to help heel the boat, reducing the draft to get her off.

'Stay still,' Uncle Jim hissed. 'Keep sounding, and add nine inches to the depth. Carry on helming, Liz, and I'll go on tweaking these sails.'

So we sat there, aground, and stopped, playing like we weren't, while *Mary*, just ahead, was afloat but not quite stopped, and *Victoria* and *Flora*, who had now picked up a strong favourable eddy, forged along inshore of us, confident that they had water, and that they could overtake us.

The ploy worked. *Victoria* lurched to a halt, well

and truly on the putty, her bow level with Aunt Liz. To avoid riding over her counter and driving right up the mud, *Flora* did a panic gybe which wrapped the kite round the forestay and took them into the tide, which carried them back up the Lynher.

Uncle Jim was delighted. 'I saw that done once before in the Solent – didn't believe it could work again. Come on, let's get after *Mary*.'

The tide had risen a few more centimetres, and it only took a slight list to port to get us off and moving over the ground again, making painfully slow ground on *Mary*.

We stuck on her tail as we worked our way up the eddy and into the main Tamar tide that would take us up river above the bridges for the last two legs. There was another short reach across the river from west to east, both buoys to be left to starboard, before the final short beat back to the finish, the same line we had started on. This run was slow even with the tide, but took immense concentration. They might be sailing old boats, but these people were highly competitive, and knew all (well, nearly all) the tricks, so we were unable to overtake *Mary*, and in spite of all Aunt Liz' efforts we were just short of establishing an overlap before the second to last mark. *Victoria* had come off the putty shortly after us, and was about 100 metres astern. Poor old *Flora* had lost a lot of ground, and was a good 200 metres astern of her, but still trying hard. The tide was running out of steam, and getting round the leeward mark first would have a double advantage.

'Take him up to windward, Liz,' Uncle Jim decided. 'We'll either get an overlap, or force him into a bad buoy rounding, and then have him at the beginning of the beat.'

She tempted him by luffing, exposing him to the danger of us getting an overlap to windward. He had little choice but to respond. Then she settled back on his stern – still no overlap, so we tried again, and again. By now we were well to windward of the straight line between the two buoys, and getting close to the end of the leg. The time had come to abandon this tactic. Aunt Liz bore away around *Mary*'s stern, to set herself up for a good buoy rounding. But it was too late for *Mary*, who had to bear away hard just to get round it, so they were forced to get onto the new course late, leaving us a great gap.

'Approach 'em wide, and leave 'em close,' said Uncle Jim as we swept past the mark on starboard, a second or few after *Mary*, but close hauled and sailing as fast as the breeze would let us.

Mary's close approach and wide departure had lost her ground, and she had not weathered the last of a line of barges moored in the stream, so she had tacked.

'Got her,' crowed Aunt Liz.

'Starboard,' Uncle Jim roared.

With a lousy buoy rounding, and having to throw in a quick tack to avoid the barge, *Mary*'s crew had not been paying attention, and we caught them by surprise. She had hardly gathered way again after the tack when the helmsman had to put the helm hard down. The jib was let fly, and then backed to get her head round in time. She was stopped in the water as we forged past – no risk of being lee-bowed that time. Poor *Mary* – worse was to follow. As soon as they had sorted themselves out, *Victoria*, who with no one else to mess them about had taken the shortest and fastest route across the river, came sweeping round the mark just as we had, and caught them too. There might even have been a knock, but Uncle Jim called my attention back to tending my jib sheet.

With all the confusion behind us, there was no way we could be caught and we were very emphatically first over the line to take the gun, and wild hoots on *Evenstar*'s fog horn. Even David and Mike had made their way to the finish in *Red Dragon*, and made their contribution to the din.

6

We put *Maud* back on her mooring, and David gave us a lift back to the yacht club in *Red Dragon*, arriving as Carol finished securing *Evenstar*. She'd anchored her off the beach, with a line to the shore, which when pulled as tight as the others could manage brought her into shallow enough water to wade ashore. Uncle Jim thought she'd be OK for perhaps an hour, so we could have lunch and a drink without bothering too much about the boat.

The yacht club bar was crammed. Mr Brothers was so delighted that the yard's boat had won and the honour of the firm been upheld that you'd have thought he had done it himself. But he was celebrating properly, with champagne, and as crew, I managed to get a glass before anyone remembered I was too young. I think I could get to quite like champagne. After that it got a little dull, although just observing can sometimes be quite fun.

Aunt Liz had bought *Hermione*'s helmsman a beer and was flirting outrageously with him, even more so as Uncle Jim was determined not to appear to have noticed. Thinking back to Sue Sawyer's visit, I couldn't but conclude that life can be made very complicated when you're old. But they seem to enjoy it. We were allowed to take *Evenstar* back when the tide had fallen to the extent that we were going to have to shift the anchor anyway, and Aunt Liz and

Uncle Jim followed some time later in a taxi, still in very high spirits.

Amazingly enough, also in high spirits when he found out about our famous victory was Mr Pascoe. He turned up with Jean-Pierre on the Wednesday, having sailed back with him from Brest.

We noticed that *Ariel* was back on one of Pascoe and Brothers' moorings on the way back from a trip up the river – we'd been up the Tavy, looking at Bere Ferrers – looking a little tatty, we thought. Mike Carter thought so too. He had been out with David in *Red Dragon* and they had seen them come in.

'Did you notice *Ariel*'s not her original name?' he asked. 'The paint's starting to peel, and you can see where the old name's been covered up. She used to be the *Tante Marie,* he's painted over *Tante Ma,* and added a big A at the beginning and an L to the end.'

We were in the Thomsons' garden leaning on the wall, doing very little. Suddenly Mike seized Judy's hands and set off with her in a Gay Gordons, singing 'Tanty Mary had a canary, up the leg of her drawers.'

Judy stamped on his foot. 'I'm sure the rest's rude. That'll do, thank you.'

'You're right,' giggled Carol, finishing the rhyme off, and getting a very old-fashioned look from Judy.

'*Tante Marie* rings a bell for some reason,' Mike said. 'But I can't think why. It'll probably come back to me at two in the morning – I'll give you a ring.'

'So long as you don't expect thanks,' Uncle Jim laughed. 'Perhaps we should ask Jean-Pierre why he did it. I think that's him in the dinghy coming round the corner.'

He dug out a pair of binoculars and confirmed that Jean-Pierre was indeed coming up river to us, and with Mr Pascoe.

'I suppose he's come to moan about what I'm charging him for the stuff on the Lynher 35s. Liz, company coming, dig out some beers please,' he called out.

Mr Pascoe had not come to moan. He had come to congratulate us on winning last weekend. It was only the urgency of his business in France that had forced him to miss the race, in which *Maud* had raced every year for the 60-odd years. And he was delighted that not only had his boat made it to the start, but had also won. This was quite a different man – he was chatty and relaxed, and listened attentively to the story of the race.

Jean-Pierre told us that this was his last trip to this side of the Channel this season. He was leaving the next evening, so this was possibly goodbye. Then he suggested that we might like to come too. There was plenty of room; we could have the after cabin again, and the men would have the saloon. Aunt Liz was obviously not invited – just as well she had unbreakable appointments at the end of the week. After a hurried discussion it was agreed that we would meet *Ariel* in the marina in Plymouth after we'd finished working; Uncle Jim would come down in *Evenstar* and leave her in the marina. The five of us would come back on the ferry from Roscoff on Sunday night or Monday morning. We sent them on their way with many thanks, and still Mr Pascoe was cheerful.

We had to work the next morning – we had fallen behind a bit, and a long weekend out crossing the Channel was not going to help. Aunt Liz dropped us at the library – she was not that upset about not going.

'Jean-Pierre is OK, but ... Anyway, you'll be all

right with Jim. Enjoy yourselves, and bring me back some pâté.'

With that she left us. We weren't feeling that enthusiastic. Notwithstanding the need to get on with tackling railway expansion, we wasted some time chatting to Mrs Carstairs, who we were surprised to find raced a 420 with her husband, so was keen for a blow-by-blow account of *Maud*'s win at the weekend. Work, fortunately, when we got down to it was not too dull – did you know they changed the width of railway track for the whole area in a single weekend?

Four o'clock finally arrived. Mrs Carstairs was happy for us to leave our work behind when we had finished, for Aunt Liz to collect on the way home – we had not looked forward to lugging it all the way backwards and forwards across the Channel; besides, we might have been tempted to do some. We packed everything away, stuffed it behind the librarian's desk, picked up our rucksacks and walked down to the Barbican.

Jean-Pierre met us at the gate and escorted us to *Ariel*, which was berthed on the end of one of the jetties.

'Your uncle Jim is getting sorted out in the main saloon – take all your things down to the after cabin, and we can leave straight away,' he said.

I followed the others down the little companionway to the tiny four-berth cabin. As I was standing on the second step down waiting for a bit of room to complete my descent, I felt a foot in the small of my back, and then I was catapulted forward on top of the others. We all collapsed in a struggling heap of arms and legs.

'Hey!' I heard Judy call out crossly. But before I could explain that I'd been pushed, and demand an explanation from Jean-Pierre, a small, hissing metal canister landed in the middle of us. I took a breath, the cabin did one or two rapid circuits around me, and then I blacked out.

We all came round more or less together as it was getting dark. *Ariel* was under way, motoring through a thick mist we could see through the scuttles, over a smooth oily sea.

'Where am I?' Carol asked. She really did – a stupid question, and so hackneyed I'd not have believed it except we were all wondering the same. We extracted our own limbs from the tangle and sat on the two lower bunks, none of us feeling too good. I tried the door – it was locked.

'What the hell is going on?' Judy demanded. She hammered on the door. 'Let us out of here. Jean-Pierre, where are you.'

In answer, the door was unlocked, and kicked open with enough force to knock Judy back into the cabin; unusually, it opened inwards. Uncle Jim had commented on it being un-seamanlike when we went to Newton Ferrers. We stared, open-mouthed, at Mr Pascoe standing in the open doorway, with a gun in his hand. He came into the cabin, grinning with unpleasant smugness.

'You are probably wondering what is going on,' he said. That was the understatement of the year. 'It will help if you know, you'll make less trouble that way. You are all being taken to North Africa, where we expect to make a handsome profit out of you.'

'Slavery?' Judy gasped incredulously. 'You have got to be joking.'

'Not at all. My family has been in the business for years. We would not normally have lifted four of you at once; girls alone on holiday are much safer.

But you were getting rather too inquisitive, and had to go. I could, of course, have just arranged a nasty accident, but Jean-Pierre thought that did not make business sense, and we should process you like the others.'

'So those stories that Jason wanted to do for the *Sentinel* were true?' asked a shocked Christine.

'Indeed.' He nodded.

'And it was your great-grandfather or whatever, and not Daniel Rogers, that used the original *Ariel* as a slaver.' I had a flash of inspiration.

'Bravo, I knew you'd guess it sooner or later. Proves me right again. My great-great-grandfather and Jean-Pierre's, who ran a foundry in Brest and was able to make the leg-irons and manacles without anyone knowing, had made a packet out of shipping blacks to the Southern states before the Civil War. They'd had a bit of a lean time after that, until someone in Brazil made them an offer they couldn't refuse. *Ariel* paid for herself several times over on the South American run, before they transferred her to the Indian and Pacific Ocean trade.'

'Jean-Pierre's great-great-grandfather,' Judy interrupted. 'That invoice we found in the old accounts – it was staring us in the face. So you and Jean-Pierre are sort of carrying on the family business? You're sickening.' She made to go for him, but he lifted the gun.

'You may think so. Please don't try anything. You're worthless to me dead, and believe me, there is no fate worse than death. In fact, if you're lucky you could have an enjoyable and lively existence. Look, it is in the very nature of mankind to dominate others; this has been the way of the world since we came down out of the trees.'

I told him to cut the philosophy – he wasn't going to talk us into going willingly. But he would not be drawn on exactly what was to happen after we arrived in France.

'So what happened to your great-great-grandfather's partner?' Christine wanted to know.

Pascoe senior appears to have been an even nastier piece of work than his descendant. Aware that Rogers had had some suspicion that *Ariel* might not be destined for the banana trade, he had been persuaded to come on the maiden voyage to see for himself. On the first night out, he and his sons had been murdered by Pascoe's paid hands, who had then sailed on to Brest, where the leg-irons were fitted, and thence to the West African coast. Judy was right; it was sickening.

'And I suppose you've sent Uncle Jim on some wild goose chase to get him out of the way. I don't imagine you two heroes go around tackling anyone big enough to fight back,' Carol sneered at him.

'I imagine he was pretty wild, and he may even have flown a little, but both for only a very short period of time,' Pascoe laughed. 'You know how proud he is of the reliability of his outboard – always starts first pull, never needs priming. When he gave it its first pull this afternoon, that will have been his last. I connected a lead to a spark plug, and wired it onto the petrol tank in the after locker, and left the lid off. One spark, and boom, the whole back end of the boat will have been blown to smithereens. So don't imagine he'll be coming to your rescue.'

'You can't expect to get away with this. Aunt Liz will tell the police, and they're bound to connect our disappearance with your absence.'

'Wrong again. I am at this moment driving up the

M6, and I shall spend the next few days with a very good friend in Scotland before visiting a boatyard on Monday. Of course, I will have flown into Glasgow airport by then, using a false passport. Jean-Pierre is not, of course, Jean-Pierre, and *Ariel* is not, of course, *Ariel*. None of us exist, and with this fog we have all literally disappeared off the face of the earth. 'Now excuse me, I must navigate. As you know, Jean-Pierre is a little lax in these matters, and we have a rendezvous to make. He will bring you something to eat in a while. And don't think of trying anything funny.' He reinforced his warning by pointing the gun at each of us, and left.

We sat down in a stunned silence. I had this horrible empty feeling in the pit of my stomach – a mixture of fear, and hopelessness, and loss. Carol broke the silence.

'He can't have blown up Uncle Jim.' Tears rolled down her face; we were all close to tears.

Christine didn't think the plan would work, but Judy thought she'd read of a killing by the IRA using the same method on a car. And that was enough to set us all off. Once we'd had a good cry, though, we stopped feeling sorry for ourselves and started feeling angry. We talked about whether to try and escape, and whether the risk was worth it.

Finally we decided that Pascoe was wrong, that there are things worse than death, and that the risk of serious injury to one of us was acceptable if we were to get out, and bring those two barbarians to justice. How to do it was the problem – we knew none of us was strong enough to overpower either one of them, even unarmed.

'We need a weapon of some sort. What about sailing knives?' Christine asked. We checked our pockets: our clasp knives were gone. Carol, however, did have a Swiss Army knife in the bottom of her rucksack, but as she only carried it for the gadgets, we were none of us convinced that we'd be able to do any damage before we came to harm. Judy pulled out some of the blades and gadgets.

'Pliers,' she said. 'If we did get one of them, we could at least pull out their fingernails.'

'Gimme, gimme, gimme,' Carol interrupted her. She grabbed the knife and disappeared into the loo. Two minutes later she reappeared with the handle from the pump, half a metre of solid brass, with a nice handle to grip. She hefted it in one hand. 'What a brilliant club,' she said. 'When Jean-Pierre comes in, wallop. Then we get the gun, and shoot the pair of them.'

'It had better be me. I'm left-handed, and if I stand there,' Christine indicated the head of the port bunk, away from where the door swung, 'I'll be close enough, and he'll probably not be thinking of danger coming from someone's left hand. People generally don't.' Christine is a useful member of the school fencing team, so she probably knew what she was talking about.

Before we had a chance for second thoughts, the key turned in the lock, and Jean-Pierre kicked the door open. Christine had barely enough time to hide the handle behind the lee-board of the upper bunk, against which she leant in a resigned and miserable pose. Jean-Pierre had the gun in his right hand, and a pan of stew and four spoons in his left.

'Dinner, ladies, is–' He got no further. Christine had been watching his eyes, she told us later, and as soon as his attention had been transferred to someone else, she moved. The loo handle smacked down his wrist, and the gun went off with a hell of a bang. I've never heard a real gun discharged in a confined space before – it's nothing like the *putt* you get from the .22s on the range at school. But Christine had planned her move and the shock of the noise did not put her off. Using both hands, she swung the handle up in a beautiful backhander that caught Jean-Pierre right on the nose. His head flicked back, and he was already dropping like a stone as her second backhanded chop hit him across the throat. He lay there motionless, making horrible gurgling noises, and for a moment we were all stunned. I don't think Christine had really been prepared for the effect her blows would have – after all, in fencing, a judge tells you if you've hit or been hit; you don't have what looks suspiciously like a dead or dying man at your feet.

We nearly blew it then. If Pascoe had had another gun – believe it or not, we had not considered the possibility that they might have one each – we'd have had it. He appeared at the top of the companionway, looked around and took one step inside. That broke the spell. Judy dived for the gun, and Pascoe left in a hurry, but not without shutting, locking and bolting the door. He only just got away with that. Judy had grabbed the gun, but never having fired a large-calibre automatic before, she was unprepared for its weight and the recoil. Her bullet did not even hit the door.

As the echoes of the enormous bang, and the fumes, died away, we looked at each other. 'What now?' someone asked.

This question was not easily answered, but after some debate we concluded that Pascoe was unlikely to try a re-entry, even with his friends once he'd reached the rendezvous. Equally, we couldn't get to him. So inactivity was forced on us. Judy continued to cover the door with the pistol, while the rest of us sorted Jean-Pierre out. He was not dead, but not very well either – he was unconscious, his breathing shallow and difficult, and his pulse weak. We put him on one of the lower bunks in the coma position, and tied his thumbs to handy fittings with the draw cords from his yellow wellies – we didn't want him coming round and being a nuisance, unlikely though that might have been.

Our attempt to use Jean-Pierre's condition as a bargaining counter with Pascoe was a failure. 'So what? He can rot down there with you,' was his response when we described of his condition and asserted that he'd die if we didn't get him to hospital. I didn't like the sound of that. I knew Pascoe was fond of melodramatic clichés, but I could see no reason for thinking we were likely to rot in the cabin.

For some time we were aware that the boat's motion had changed. There was no change in the light outside – the fog and twilight combined in a uniform gloom – but it seemed that the swell was coming from the port side instead of the starboard bow. Then the engine stopped, and there was an awful lot of banging and clanging from forward.

'He'll have to let us out soon,' said Judy. 'I bet he can't manage this without an engine on his own. What luck the engine conking out.'

'I'm not so sure.' Carol knew something about engines – she had had the task of writing the engine log, and dipping the oil and things like that when Uncle Jim had his Hillyard. 'It didn't sound like it was conking out. It did that *chunka chunka, whirr, tunk tunk* rattle that Uncle Jim's used to do when you stopped it normally.'

She was right. After about five minutes we heard the powerful diesel restart. 'Possibly a cooling water problem,' Carol surmised. 'Weed in the inlet maybe.'

There was more thumping about on deck, and then the unmistakable sound of an outboard being started and roaring into life. As the racket faded, Judy looked out of the cabin scuttle.

'Look, he's off. Where's he going and why? I'm going to take a pot at him.' But she couldn't shift the clamps on the scuttle fast enough, and Mr Pascoe and the inflatable disappeared into the deepening gloom.

'Time we got ourselves out of here,' Carol pronounced, squinting at the keyhole. 'Let's see if the old pencil and paper trick works.'

To everyone's astonishment, it did. She used another of the tools on her Swiss Army knife that had never appeared to have any useful function before to move the key into position, and poke it out, where it fell onto a sheet of scrap computer paper I had brought, just in case we wanted to do some work. It didn't bounce into the bilge, and the gap under the door was big enough to let it through. Triumphantly, Carol unlocked the door. But of course it wouldn't open because it was bolted on the outside.

'C'mon,' said Christine, 'out of the way, let's get some brute force on it.' She had picked up the handle from the loo, and by pulling the door as far back as we could she managed to get it in the gap and start levering. She even succeeded in ripping a bit of the door off.

It was Carol who spotted the problem. 'It must be a whopping great bolt. Look, it's secured by these nuts here.' Indeed it was through-bolted to the door, not just screwed, and Carol's trusty knife could not cope with the nuts.

'Stand back, I'll blow it off.' Judy took aim, and blasted a hole in the wood about fifteen centimetres away from the bolt. Her next shot did the trick. The whole top corner of the door, and a bit of the frame disappeared. I suppose it was a bit risky – after all, the bullet could have bounced back, but they never do in the films, so it never occurred to us at the time.

Ears still ringing from the two enormous bangs, we staggered into the cockpit. *Ariel* had a strange motion – a slow roll. She'd sort of slump to one side, stagger upright, and then slump over to the other side. It made the water in the bilges slosh about a bit too – the significance of which had not struck us while we were busy getting out of the after cabin. It struck Christine, though, who was last out, as a tide of rather nasty water lapped over the cabin sole.

'We're sinking!' she shrieked.

Carol kicked open the main cabin door. 'You're right,' she said. 'This end's sinking too.' She staggered back as a cloud of smoke belched out of the open door.

'And on fire. Let's get out of here.' Christine was, understandably, getting hysterical.

'Rubbish, that's just exhaust smoke. Easy to stop that.' Carol flipped up the cover on the engine controls and pulled the stop switch. *'Chunka chunka, whirr, tunk tunk, rattle,'* she said as the engine did just that, and was silent. 'Now where's the seacock? Uncle Jim's was down here.'

She lifted a portion of the cockpit floor and reached down into the bilge. She grunted a few times, and stood up wiping her hands on her jeans with satisfaction. 'Just the same, and just as stiff, but that's done it.'

'Come on, let's get pumping,' I urged. 'Christine, you remember how it worked?' We had all had a go on our trip to the Yealm, and I reckoned that it would do her good to have something to do.

Carol had put her head into the main cabin, and quickly withdrew it. 'Difficult to tell, it's dark, and there are a lot of fumes, but I reckon that banging we heard was him knocking the exhaust off the manifold, so as the engine was running it was pumping cooling water straight into the bilge. If she's settled much, the exhaust outlet will be under water too, so we'll have to block that, and he may have opened the cocks and taken the pipes off the loo and the sink. Someone's got to go down there, and it had better be me, 'cos no one else knows what they're looking for. Right?'

I thought she was very brave, and had to admit she was right too.

'Can't we open the forward hatch?' Judy asked as she swung with Christine on the bilge pump. 'That will help disperse the fumes, and you ought to have a line on you, so we can pull you out if the fumes get too much.'

That was good thinking. Fortunately, the fore hatch was not bolted on the inside. There was a very light breeze from over the port quarter, which pushed the smoke out forward. Carol put a bowline round her waist on the end of the main sheet, and descended into the dark, knee-deep water.

'Keep talking, Carol,' I urged. Then I could tell if she was getting groggy, or even passed out.

'OK. One, two, three. I'm going to open the scuttle

first, so I can take a breath if I can't fix it first time. Yes, here it is.' She had been right. Pascoe had bashed the exhaust off the engine. Closing the seacock and turning off the engine had stopped one source of water, but more was pouring in through the exhaust pipe every time *Ariel* rolled.

Carol took a deep breath from the open scuttle. 'It's horrible down here. If I wasn't so frightened, and it wasn't so important, I think I'd be sick,' she said. 'I'm going to try and bend this pipe up above the water level.' She bent down and heaved. 'That was easier than I expected. Not perfect, but better. Right, another breath, and then the heads.'

I heard her wade forward, still counting. She opened the door to the heads compartment up forward, and called out that the cocks had in fact been opened and the plastic pipe cut. Fortunately, the lead outlet pip had proved too difficult so it was a relatively small leak, quickly stopped as she shut the valve.

'I'll just check the sink. One, two, three.' She came back. 'The air's a lot clearer, but this water's blooming cold. Pump faster, you two,' she shouted. The sink drain was a little more difficult. The valve was solid, and the handle sheered off in Carol's hand, but she found an old wine cork bobbing around and stuffed that in the end of the cut pipe.

'The fumes have all gone,' she said. 'And you know what Uncle Jim says is the best sort of bilge pump, don't you?'

'A frightened man with a bucket,' I replied. 'Or in this case, two girls. Do you want to bail, or chuck?'

Carol reckoned that as she was wet, she might just as well stay below. She found a couple of large pans and between us we started heaving water over the side. If *Ariel* had had a self-draining cockpit we'd have been faster, but we still shifted a fair volume of water, while Judy and Christine kept up the good work on the semi-rotary pump.

It was dark by the time we'd made enough progress for Carol to be finding it difficult to fill the pans. She decided she would be better employed trying to get some lights working.

'The batteries must be OK. If they'd been flooded they'd have produced lots of nasty gases, I think – I'm glad I didn't think of that until just now.' She grinned. I hadn't realised until then what a good egg my cousin is.

I went aft and dug around in my rucksack for my torch. Jean-Pierre was still unconscious; he looked in a bad way. Still, better than drowned, I thought, perhaps a little heartlessly. By torchlight, Carol found the switches and soon had every light that worked blazing – there was the remote possibility that someone might be looking for us. Then she made some tea.

'Yuk,' she said, 'sea water's got into the fresh. Still, better than nothing. I wonder if there's anything to eat.'

'Carol, how can you think of your stomach?' Christine demanded. 'We've got to get out of here.'

'How?' she replied. 'No wind; engine's bust. All we can do is wait for some wind, then sail north until we sight land, and then turn left or right.'

'I suppose we could flash SOS on all the lights. Someone might see us,' Judy suggested.

'Or we could try the radio,' I said, noticing the shiny new VHF set for the first time.

'Good grief, that wasn't there last time we were on board. Aren't we dumb? I should have seen it, I've been down here longest,' Carol admitted. 'Bags I have first go.'

A demand we all agreed to – she was probably the only one able to get it going.

The search for food abandoned, Carol tinkered with the set, while the rest of us looked for an instruction manual. We found it, soggy pulp in a corner.

'Never mind. I've watched David playing with one he fitted in *Red Dragon*. I reckon I've got it. Here we go. Mayday, mayday, mayday, this is yacht *Ariel*, yacht *Ariel*, yacht *Ariel*. What on earth do I say next?' she asked.

There was no need to answer. As soon as she took her finger off the transmit button, we heard, 'Yacht *Ariel*, this is *Red Dragon*, are you OK?'

'Uncle Jim, you're alive, what are you doing here?' Any pretence at radio procedure was forgotten as Carol screeched delightedly at the mike.

'*Ariel*, *Red Dragon*, this is Brixham Coastguard, rescue co-ordination, can we get *Ariel*'s position fixed first?'

'We don't know where we are.'

'In that case tell me your condition, and we can get a fix on your transmission. Talk for about thirty seconds.'

Carol did, ending lamely with 'Over, was that all right?'

Very quickly the coastguard gave us our position, and told us that a customs launch was closest to us, and would be with us in about 15 minutes.

'Can't we talk to Uncle Jim, please?' she asked.

He came back on the air long enough to tell us that he was fine, that he'd see us soon, and that we ought to get off the air and let the coastguard get on with dismantling the search operation.

'No, they musn't do that,' Carol interrupted.

'Someone has to find Pascoe – he's getting away in the rubber dinghy.' She explained that he'd been gone about two hours, but that didn't seem to upset anyone. We discovered why very quickly as a jet roared overhead. The coastguard explained that it was the RAF Nimrod that had fixed our position from our radio transmission, and had us on radar. By playing back the tapes of his radar for the last couple of hours there was a reasonable chance of backtracking our echo now they knew which it was, and then picking up the direction Pascoe had gone. Small though it is, it seems even an outboard motor can be detected.

'Now that you've given away all our secrets, perhaps we can get on with guiding the customs to the target,' a rather plummy voice broke in. It was all surprisingly relaxed.

Judy wanted to know if we should let off a flare as she'd found a box of them in a locker in the cockpit, but there was no need as the customs could already see our lights.

They were soon alongside. We were taken on board and given some very welcome non-salty tea. Jean-Pierre was taken off in a stretcher. Then, with *Ariel* in tow, we set off towards Plymouth.

Because Jean-Pierre was in such a bad condition, they decided that he needed hospital quickly, and a helicopter was soon on its way to take him off. They didn't take us too, which was a bit disappointing, but you could see why. The transfer – high-line transfer, they called it – looked rather hairy, and took time, which was something Jean-Pierre did not have much of. So we were left on board, making statements and, in Carol's case at least, tucking into eggs and bacon before falling fast asleep in the tiny saloon.

Red Dragon, with David, Michael and Uncle Jim on board, met us off Plymouth breakwater at four o'clock in the morning, just as it was getting light. The fog had gone, blown away by a light north westerly. We waved and shouted to each other, but it wasn't possible to have a coherent conversation; that had to wait until we were alongside in the Barbican. Even then we'd not have had a chance to tell Uncle Jim what had happened, nor to find out how he'd survived Pascoe's attempt to blow him up, and why he was out in *Red Dragon* with everyone else looking for us, if he hadn't talked his way into the police van which was waiting to whisk us away from the crowd of reporters on the jetty.

'Poor old Jason, he was right all along, and now he thinks he's lost his scoop to me. Perhaps you girls will give an interview when the police have finished,' he said.

We groaned at the thought of more statements, but it seemed that our little escapade had just revealed the tip of the iceberg, and the police were very interested in everything we could remember about Jean-Pierre and Pascoe's indiscretions when they thought they were safe. There was also the question of Jean-Pierre's injuries – he was in intensive care, and even if we were not going to be held to blame, careful enquiries had to be made to ensure we had not overstepped the line of self-defence.

'Load of rubbish, in my view,' Uncle Jim grumbled. 'You should have chucked him over the side.'

Then he told us his story. He had rowed out to *Evenstar* to motor down to meet us as arranged, and was about to take his usual hefty pull on the outboard starting cord, when it occurred to him to check he had enough fuel. We had played about with the boat so much that he had no idea how much there was. He was somewhat surprised to find that his key did not fit the padlock on the after locker (Pascoe had changed it for an identical model) and assumed that it had rusted solid and that he would have to cut it off, so he was about to motor in to the shore to get a hacksaw. It was only the news that morning of a terrorist bomb in London that made him more suspicious than usual – he had served on the anti-gun running patrol in Ireland once – and he actually checked the engine, to find an electric cable running beneath the fuel line into the locker. By now more curious than suspicious, he rowed *Evenstar* in and cut the padlock off. It was, he admitted, a spectacularly stupid thing to do. If the device had not been so amateurish, there could well have been a booby trap attached to the locker door, and then where would he have been?

As he walked back to the cottage to phone the police, the phone rang. It was Mike. He had remembered where he had seen the name *Tante Marie*. The Admiralty sends out information on suspicious vessels to ships working in coastal waters and likely to come across them, it seems – and *Tante Marie* had been on just such a signal as being stolen, and possibly used for smuggling drugs.

Thereafter, things had moved fast. The police alerted the coastguard, customs, the Navy, the RAF, and anybody else who might help, and a massive search was going on when we had come up on the radio. Mike had persuaded David that they should join in, now that he had his radio fitted, and Uncle Jim had gone along to keep an eye on them – a tomfool escapade, he called it. But it had meant that they were able to hear that we were OK first-hand.

It only remained to bring Pascoe to book. This was not proving as easy as first predictions might have suggested. The RAF Nimrod's tapes were being analysed minutely ashore somewhere.

They had backtracked us, and had pinpointed when we stopped, but tracking the very poor echo from the outboard motor was difficult. Pascoe did seem to have headed south, and, we were told, they were trying to project his track, and find something with which he might have rendezvoused.

'What about the chart?' Carol asked. 'Had he written on that?'

Of course that was being checked, and of course there was writing on it, lots of it, all rubbed out. It was being tested in the police laboratory.

Statements over, we were taken back to Saltash in two police cars, which was rather fun as we persuaded them to put the siren on and blast down the dual carriageway. Not legal, but nothing was too much trouble for people who had given a white slaver his just desserts. Our driver had a clear concept of right and wrong in this case! In Saltash, as promised, we gave Jason his exclusive before getting tidied up for the press conference proper.

That was rather a bore. I had expected it to be more exciting, being the focus of so much attention, but most of the questions were pretty stupid, and the TV lights and flash bulbs gave us headaches. It was nice to see Sue Sawyer again, though – she was the only one not to talk down to us. However, she left us with one disturbing question. Having established that Pascoe was indeed a nasty piece of work, were we not frightened that he was still at large?

That aspect had not occurred to us. We had assumed

that once he'd started running he'd have carried on, and gone to ground.

The idea that he might want revenge was novel and worrying.

In fact it worried me so much that I couldn't sleep that night. The phone rang at about two in the morning, and as it was answered I knew someone else was up, so I crept downstairs. It was Uncle Jim.

'Hi,' he said. 'Can't sleep?' I nodded.

'Make us some tea then, and I'll tell you what that phone call was about, and if you want, you can talk.'

It was the police phoning. He told me Jean-Pierre was out of immediate danger, and they hoped to be able to question him in a day or so. The French police had met the fishing boat which the RAF had identified as crossing and stopping on Pascoe's track – that had taken a lot of electronic detective work, and a bit of luck. Everyone was hopeful that they had got the next link in the chain, but the fishing boat was clean, no sign of Pascoe or manacles or anything like that. French Navy divers even checked under the hull – all they found was a bit of rope and a piece of neoprene around the prop shaft.

The boat's skipper admitted that they had stopped that night – something had caught on the prop – but after they'd poked about with a broom all seemed clear and they'd carried on. The implication was that they'd not seen Pascoe in the fog – he'd have been taking care not to be seen – and run him down, and that was the end of him. I accepted that and happily returned to bed.

An inquest a few weeks later accepted it too, and it does seem the most likely thing to have happened – but I do sometimes wonder.

The project? With all the excitement and aftermath

of being kidnapped, we lost lots of time and had to abandon sailing to get it done on time. But Mr Brothers was as good as his word, and David did a brilliant job of turning it into something special. As a collaborative effort, it was barred from winning any prizes at school, but better than that by far was that the copy we gave to the local library proved so popular that a Plymouth publishing firm brought it out in their series of local history books. There's real fame for you, having your name on W. H. Smith's shelves – much better than some old cup that no one ever notices. Oh, and they gave us money too, so all in all, it was a pretty good summer holiday.